"I have no doubt you have plenty of male admirers fighting for your attention."

"Not so many." Most of the men she knew weren't her biggest fans. Not anymore. But then Mike didn't need to know that. "I lead a pretty boring life, in fact."

"I would have to disagree with you there." One of his hands came up, fingers sliding into the hair at her nape. "Most of my encounters with you have been anything but boring."

True. And most of those encounters had ended up with her falling into his arms. Literally, at times. And once it had ended up with him kissing her.

The memory of that frantic session in the barn washed over her. She wanted that again...wanted his lips on hers—wanted to forget about the horrors of this afternoon, even if just for a few minutes.

As if he'd read her mind he tilted her head back until their eyes met. He stared at her for several long seconds, as if seeking confirmation of something. Then slowly, far too slowly, his head lowered until his lips touched hers. A shard of longing went through her. This was how it was supposed to be between a man and woman: an attraction that built until there was no denying it on either side. At least not on hers. She was attracted. Had been almost from the moment she'd set eyes on him.

Dear Reader

There have been times in my life when I've jokingly said, 'I wish I could start all over again—change my name, my location…go someplace where no one knows who I am.' That got me thinking. What if, for reasons not of my choosing, I *had* to do all those things? What if I wound up in the wrong place at the wrong time and my life was put in danger—or the lives of my loved ones? Could I do it? Give up everything and assume a new identity?

That's what hippotherapist Trisha Bolton must do when she enters a witness protection programme and finds herself in a new town with a brand-new name. She's not allowed any contact with those from her past and has learned the hard way that it's better not to trust anyone—not even neurologist Mike Dunning, whose quiet intensity puts her on guard from their very first meeting. Yes, there are sparks erupting between them, but it's better not to become too attached—because at any moment her past might just catch up with her.

Thank you for joining Trisha and Mike as they navigate the waters of trust and betrayal and learn the true meaning of new beginnings. I hope you enjoy reading about these very special characters as much as I loved writing about them.

Love

Tina Beckett

HIS GIRL
FROM NOWHERE

BY
TINA BECKETT

First published in Great Britain 2014
by Mills & Boon, an imprint of Harlequin (UK) Limited,
Eton House, 18-24 Paradise Road, Richmond, Surrey, TW9 1SR

© 2014 Tina Beckett

ISBN: 978-0-263-24387-1

Harlequin (UK) Limited's policy is to use papers that are natural, renewable and recyclable products and made from wood grown in sustainable forests. The logging and manufacturing processes conform to the legal environmental regulations of the country of origin.

Printed and bound in Great Britain
by CPI Antony Rowe, Chippenham, Wiltshire

Born to a family that was always on the move, **Tina Beckett** learned to pack a suitcase almost before she knew how to tie her shoes. Fortunately she met a man who also loved to travel, and she snapped him right up. Married for over twenty years, Tina has three wonderful children and has lived in gorgeous places such as Portugal and Brazil.

Living where English reading material is difficult to find has its drawbacks, however. Tina had to come up with creative ways to satisfy her love for romance novels, so she picked up her pen and tried writing one. After her tenth book she realised she was hooked. She was officially a writer.

A three-time Golden Heart finalist, and fluent in Portuguese, Tina now divides her time between the United States and Brazil. She loves to use exotic locales as the backdrop for many of her stories. When she's not writing you can find her either on horseback or soldering stained glass panels for her home.

Tina loves to hear from readers. You can contact her through her website or 'friend' her on Facebook.

Recent titles by Tina Beckett:

Dedication

To my three children. Each of your births
marked a new beginning. I love you very much.

**Praise for
Tina Beckett:**

'…a tension-filled, emotional story
with just the right amount of drama. The author's
vivid description of the Brazilian jungle and its people
make this story something special.'
—*RT Book Reviews* on
DOCTOR'S GUIDE TO DATING IN THE JUNGLE

'Medical romance lovers will definitely like
NYC ANGELS: FLIRTING WITH DANGER by
Tina Beckett, for who doesn't like a
good forbidden romance…?'
—*HarlequinJunkie.com*

CHAPTER ONE

SOMEONE WAS IN her barn.

At least, according to her horse's soft nicker there was. Balancing the bay gelding's right rear hoof on her thigh, Trisha Bolton paused, the curved metal pick in her hand coming to a halt as she listened. Great. It had taken a couple of firm nudges to get Brutus to lift that last leg so she could finish scraping the debris from the bottoms of his hooves. She didn't want to signal she was done until she actually was. Because she doubted he'd co-operate a second time—even for a chunk of carrot.

Brutus snuffed, a huge exhalation of sound, and shifted his weight. Maybe he was just impatient to be let out to graze with the other horses.

"Steady, boy." She readjusted her grip so his hoof didn't slide down her thigh and drop onto her foot. "We're almost done."

"Hello?" she called out, just in case. "I'm over in the cross ties."

No one responded.

She frowned as she caught the soft sound of footsteps at the far end of the concrete aisle between the stalls, heading her way. So there *was* someone here. The shoes were quiet, making little sound, each step planted carefully. Not rubber-soled quiet like a tennis shoe, but not the defined click of a riding boot either.

Five miles south of Dusty Hills, Nevada, her little chunk of land lay at the very end of a quarter-mile dirt track. Not the kind of place someone just happened upon. If you found her operation, it was because you came looking for it. And she didn't have a client at all today, which meant…

Oh, Lord. Roger?

She swallowed hard, then forced herself to relax. No, he'd been moved to Virginia. Would be there for a very long time, according to the courts.

Today was their third anniversary, though. It would be just like him to reach out and remind her that he was still a part of her world, no matter how many miles separated them.

Brutus would be able to see whoever was here from his position at the front of the stall. Trisha, however, still hunched over his back hoof, had her choice of two lovely views: the slatted back wall of the grooming area or her horse's muscular backside. She could take her pick.

She tried again. "Who's there? Larry?"

Her barn helper wasn't scheduled to muck out the stalls again until tomorrow morning. And Penny was out at a supply fair, hoping to score a new bareback pad for those of their patients who had better control over their motor skills. And, besides, both of her workers knew enough to make their presence known when they came through those barn doors. As did all of her clients. There was even a cheerful sign to that effect over the entry beam: *Feel free to say hello!*

Fear of what could be out there still governed so many of her decisions. Most days she was okay, but today wasn't one of them.

There was still no answer to her greeting. And the footsteps were closer now. Still quiet. Stealthy, almost.

Brutus tossed his head, the clips attached to either side of his halter jingling in a way that didn't help her nerves. Her fingers tightened around the wooden handle of the hoof pick. She could always use the tool as a weapon, if need be, although the thought of cutting someone with it made her feel physically ill—reminded her too much of past events.

The agents had sworn her new identity was secure. That assurance, along with the many miles between her and her past, was supposed to ensure her safety. But she'd seen enough to know there were no guarantees—of anything—in this life.

Giving up on finishing her task, she took a step back and allowed Brutus's hoof to settle heavily on the ground. He shifted his weight onto it and tried to glance back at her, probably wondering what the heck was going on. Then his ears pricked forward, and he looked at something off to the right. She flattened her hand on his haunch, so he'd know where she was as she swiveled toward the front, keeping her body close to that of her horse. The earthy smells of fresh manure and warm animal faded away as she struggled to keep track of the sounds.

Should she call out again?

What if it was someone she didn't know? Or, worse, someone she did?

Get a grip, Trish, and think.

If it came down to it, an intruder would have to duck under one of the nylon ties that secured Brutus's head to either side of the grooming stall, giving her a few precious seconds to slip behind the animal and out the other side—preferably without getting kicked in the ribs in the process, if something startled her horse.

Like a gunshot?

"Easy, boy." The soft quaver in her voice made Brutus's moist coat twitch beneath her fingertips. He could sense her growing fear.

Why she'd decided to keep her rifle locked in a safe in the house was beyond her. No, it wasn't. She'd rather risk her own safety than that of her young patients.

She slid her hand back a few inches, tangling her fingers in the long silky strands of Brutus's tail. There were no true pain receptors in the hairs, so he wouldn't feel a thing if she had to use it to give herself some momentum to swing behind him.

If *they'd* found her, they'd target her and not her horse. At least, that was her hope.

There! A man came into view on Brutus's left, silently facing her from the other side of the aisle with dark narrowed eyes. His shoes were black. Shiny. Leather bottoms. A professional's shoes. Thick dark hair was swept back from his face, and his hands were buried in the pockets of his gray slacks. If her heart hadn't been thundering in her chest like that of a racehorse headed for the finish line, she might think the stranger was dangerously handsome.

As it was, he just looked dangerous. Hard carved lines made up his jawline. And a muscle tensed and released repeatedly in his cheek.

Terror swept over her as he withdrew a hand—empty, thank God—and motioned her out of the stall without a word.

She stayed put.

"C-can I help you?" The hand in Brutus's tail tightened into a fist as she prepared to bolt. She held the pick slightly away from her body, hoping to draw the man's attention to it and make him think twice about coming in after her. The memory of blood—too much blood—made bile rise in her throat. Could she really slash him with it?

Yes. She'd already proven she was capable of things she'd never dreamed possible.

He motioned to her again, his frown deepening as his eyes moved to the horse and then back to her.

Why didn't he say something?

If you think I'm coming out of this stall, without knowing exactly—

Her horse had had enough of the thickening tension. He pinned his ears and shied to the right, hindquarters shimmying in an arc away from her. The abrupt movement caused her to lose her grip on his tail just as he let out a shrill whinny.

It was as if a bomb had gone off. Trisha found herself flying through the air, steel bands around either arm as she tumbled through space and landed in a heap on the hard concrete outside the stall.

Scratch that. It wasn't concrete. It was a body. The steel bands: hands, which still gripped her upper arms. His breath whooshed against her ear in rhythmic gusts.

And the words coming out of his mouth... Well, those weren't sweet nothings.

So he *could* talk.

She patted the ground in a panic, searching for her hoof pick. And then her heart stopped as she saw it. Five feet above the guy's head. Too far to reach.

Her thighs were wedged between his, and she felt every hard muscle of his torso tensed and ready, but that wasn't what she was worried about. As quick as a bunny she stroked both palms over the stranger's sides, down his lean hips, and then dragged them back up the front of his thighs, feeling for any lump that wasn't a body part. Roger had taught her exactly where to look. Had made her pat down her contact. Right before he'd aimed his gun and…

She reached the man's pelvis, fingers probing, searching.

"What the hell?" The stranger flipped her over so that he was on top—weight resting on his bent elbows, strong thighs still bracketing her legs. Only now her hands were imprisoned by his on either side of her head. "Are you seriously doing this? Now? You could have been killed."

Her brain hitched. She'd thought she *was* going to be killed. By him.

There was still one place she hadn't checked. The back of his waistband. But she couldn't move. And she was having second thoughts about who'd sent him. Especially since things were beginning to show some interest at the spot where they were joined together.

Breath still sawing in and out of her lungs, she stared up at him, trying to hold perfectly still. "Who are you? And why are you here?"

One eyebrow crept up, and his frown eased. "Maybe you should have stopped to ask that before feeling me up."

Feeling him…

"Excuse me?"

This was no killer. So who was he? She licked her lips, praying he wasn't an estranged parent of one of her patients. If so, she'd definitely not made the best first impression. Then again, neither had he.

"Why didn't you say something, instead of just standing there? You scared me to death. Not to mention dragging me out of the…" She closed her eyes for a second before reopening them and glaring. "You never make sudden movements around a horse. Especially not that horse. You could have gotten us *both* killed."

The harsh dipping of something in his throat caught her attention. He stayed put for another second or two then rolled off her with a harsh oath and climbed to his feet. "Believe it or not, I was trying *not* to scare him into doing something crazy."

He held a hand toward her, but she ignored it and scrambled to her feet under her own power, hoping she looked more in control of herself than she felt. "Well, consider that a fail." She glanced at Brutus for proof, only to find him with his head hung low, lids half-shut. His nostrils flared as he huffed out a tired breath.

Really? Trisha rolled her eyes. *Thanks for backing me up there, bud. You could at least look a* little *shaken up.*

The stranger eyed the horse as well, looking more than a little wary. "I guess now's as good a time as any to ask. Are you Patricia Bolton?"

She nodded. At least he hadn't used her other name. A few more muscles came off high alert.

He continued, "Well, Ms. Bolton, despite our rather questionable introduction, it seems we share a mutual acquaintance." One of his hands shifted to the small of his back. The one place she hadn't checked.

Her brain skittered back toward panic, the blood draining from her head. "Is it Roger?" she whispered.

His gaze sharpened, and he lowered his hand, taking a step forward, only to stop when she jerked backwards. He shook his head, his eyes still focused on her face. "No, not Roger. Clara. Clara Trimble. Her mother said you were hoping to work with her. I'm Mike Dunning, the neurosurgeon who performed her operation."

Mike had seen all kinds of expressions on a woman's face as she lay beneath him—lust, need, affection, love. But never in his life had he inspired abject terror. He should have realized the hands sweeping over his body had had a quick furtive quality to them, not the slow, languorous touches he was used to. She'd been looking for something specific.

"I'm sorry I scared you." He'd been a little panicked himself when that animal had given that high-pitched shriek. His nerves had already been stretched to breaking point the second he'd set foot in the barn, and each step had made the feeling that much worse. He hadn't dared call out to her, had barely been able to push one foot in front of the other.

Mike and horses could no longer be considered friends. Not that they'd ever been particularly close. But four years and a whole lot of distance had changed nothing, it seemed. He still couldn't stand to be near them.

The woman in question gave a rough exhalation of breath, drawing the back of her hand over her brow and leaving a smudge of some dark substance that made his lips curve.

He'd tackled her to the ground, what did he expect?

"Clara," she said. "Of course. Doris said she was going to ask you to contact me. I expected a phone call, not a visit."

His brows went up, more convinced than ever that putting his patient on the back of a thousand-pound animal was a bad idea. Both the horse—and its owner—seemed strong-headed, unpredictable. He'd seen first-hand what kind of devastation that combination could cause. He curled his left hand into a loose fist, the emptiness he found there mirroring the void within his chest. "I'm not about to prescribe something for a patient I can't fully endorse."

"Oh." She bit her lip and backed up another pace or

two before dropping onto a white plastic bucket against a nearby stall door. "If you had just called first..."

"I did try. I left a message on your machine a few hours ago. I had a break and decided to stop over in person, instead of waiting for you to return my call." He turned to look at the animal behind him, expecting it to break free of its ties and grab hold of his shirt at any second. He gestured at it. "And if this is your idea of safe, then I'm afraid—"

She stood in a rush. "Brutus isn't one of my therapy horses. I can assure you the horses I use with my patients are extremely gentle and love their job. Brutus is a...special case."

Special. Yes, he could see that. About as special as its name.

He glanced around the rest of the barn, but it was empty. "So where are the other horses?"

"Out in the pasture. It's their day off. Brutus was just about to join them." She crossed over to her horse, murmuring something in a low voice before wrapping an arm under the creature's neck and leaning her temple against it.

He swallowed back a ball of fear when the big animal shifted closer to her. "Could you come away from there, please?"

Instead of doing as he asked, she leaned sideways and grabbed a loop of leather off a peg on the wall and unclipped one of the ties holding the horse in place. She replaced it with a hook from the loop in her hand. Then she unsnapped the tie on the other side.

The creature was free, except for that thin cord she held.

As if knowing exactly what he was thinking, the horse snorted and bobbed its head.

"What are you doing?"

She eyed him, a slight pucker between her brows. "I told you. Brutus needs to be turned out."

To his shock, she held the length of leather out to him. "Do you mind leading him while I take the wheelbarrow out to the compost heap?"

"I'd prefer it if you just put him in a stall." He gestured to the row of empty boxes.

She bent over to pick up the curved metal instrument she'd been using when he'd arrived. For a second or two he'd wondered if she'd planned on gutting him with it, before dismissing the idea as ridiculous. She tossed the item into a wooden chest then shrugged. "Okay. I'll lead him and *you* can take the wheelbarrow. The compost heap is on the way out to the pasture. We can talk on the way and you can see the other horses." She gave a quick laugh, seeming to have recovered her composure. "You might want to watch your shoes, though. Wouldn't want to ruin them."

He glanced to the side and saw a wheelbarrow filled with a substance he recognized, and which looked suspiciously like the smudge on Ms. Bolton's forehead. Despite the situation, he couldn't stop a smile from forming. She thought he was afraid of a little horse manure? He would have set her straight, but she was already on the move, the horse swinging out of the stall and passing within two feet of where he stood. Its hooves made a familiar clop-clop as the pair moved toward the far doors.

He rolled his eyes. The things he did for his patients.

Okay, Mike. You're a brain surgeon. You've seen a whole lot worse than this.

Yes, he had.

He curled his hands around the handles of the wheelbarrow and lifted, finding the thing surprisingly heavy.

Marcy had boarded her horses at another location, heading out there in the mornings and coming home in the evenings. He'd never had much to do with her profession. Until the night she hadn't come home at all. And he'd been left to live with the aftermath.

An aftermath that still rose up to choke him at times. Like now?

Hell. The sooner he got off Patricia Bolton's property, the better.

He caught up to her within a minute, making sure to stay on her far side, away from the horse, which trudged forward like it hadn't a care in the world. You'd never know it was the same animal who'd minutes ago caused him to charge into the pen, his only thought to drag Ms. Bolton out of harm's way.

Apparently, she hadn't needed his help after all.

"So, what set him off?" He wasn't sure why he asked. Maybe to try to understand what had happened four years ago.

She glanced at him. "The way you motioned me out of the cross ties. He's leery of arms that move in quick jerky motions. Especially if they're flicked back and then brought down in a rush."

That made him pause. "Why didn't you say something the first time I did it?" She'd just stood there and let him repeat the gesture a second time without saying a word.

"I thought you were…" She shook her head. "It's complicated. Just don't do it again."

Not much chance of that, since he'd probably never see Ms. Bolton—or Brutus—again after today. That included those deep green eyes fringed with thick dark lashes. And her cute blonde ponytail that was currently swishing back and forth with every step she took. And her extremely inviting derrière, which seemed custom made for gripping.

Tightening his fingers on the handles of the wheelbarrow and glad the metal object hid a certain wayward body part, he tried to shift his thoughts back to his patient. "So Doris Trimble thinks you can help Clara."

"I think I can too." She glanced sideways at him and then back ahead.

There was no hint of conceit or of trying to win him over to her position, just a matter-of-fact response. Did she actually expect him to take that at face value, without any substantive proof? Well, he'd just match her short response with one of his own.

"How?"

"There are studies. Testimonials—"

That word made him snort.

She drew up short and her horse halted as well, heaving a huge breath and then blowing it out with a blubber of lips, like a child irritated at being kept from his recess.

"Look, if you've already made up your mind, why are you even here?"

Good question. He could have told Clara's mother no. Or just signed off on the recommendation form that would allow insurance to cover the therapy. Or, like Patricia had said, he could have just called and had a brief conversation with her. He had tried, as he'd told her, but he couldn't bring himself to put a child in harm's way, no matter how uncomfortable coming out here might be for him. Still, she was right. He needed to extend her the same courtesy he expected to have afforded to him. He needed to hear her out.

"I want Clara to have the best treatment options, so I'm not ready to rule out anything."

"And yet when you ask me for data, you make scoffing sounds before I've said ten words."

"Fair enough. So convince me." He let the wheelbarrow's supports touch the ground and crossed his arms over his chest, waiting.

"Great." She shook her head and started back down the path without a word, the horse again moving with her.

This woman was impossible. He grabbed the handles and followed her. It was really hard to carry on an intelligent conversation while hauling a load of manure.

She held up the tip of her rope and pointed off to the left. "Dump it over there behind that wooden barricade, if you don't mind. You can leave the wheelbarrow there. Thanks."

By the time he'd done as she asked, she'd released Demon Seed—a better name than Brutus, in his opinion—into a large fenced grassy area.

Mike arrived just in time to see four other horses making a beeline for the newcomer, tails flowing out behind them as they galloped toward the fence. There was a kind of strange powwow between the animals, accompanied by various sounds, then one of the horses wheeled around and raced away from the group. The others soon followed suit. None of them looked particularly tame.

"Those are your therapy horses?"

"Yes. Brutus is the only one not used in the program."

"How do you keep them under control?"

She glanced out at the field. "They know when it's time to work and when it's time to play. I can assure you that they take their jobs as seriously as any other kind of service animal."

Was she talking about seeing-eye dogs? "But not Brutus."

"No. Not Brutus. I told you, he's a special case. The

other horses are teaching him what it means to be a..."
She shrugged. "Well, a horse. Sometimes horses—and
people—have to relearn what it means to be normal."

That was one thing on which they could both agree.
He hadn't quite made it there yet. "So tell me about your
program."

She waited for a minute then smiled. "You say you
want to know about it, but every time I start to talk you
shut yourself off."

"Sorry?"

Her fingers touched his left forearm, sending a jolt
through him. "You cross your arms. Meaning you're not
going to accept what I have to say."

He unfolded his limbs, mostly to dislodge her fingers. "Not true."

"No?"

Okay, so she was right. But he wasn't sure how to
get past it. He could stand there with his arms hanging
straight down, but it wouldn't mean a thing. He'd still be
skeptical, and he couldn't think of anything she could do
that would change the way he felt. Marcy had told him
one thing and then gone and done another. How did he
know Patricia wouldn't bend the truth to suit her own
purposes? "I guess we're at an impasse, then."

"Not quite. I think I might have a solution."

He couldn't think of one to save his life. "I'm listening." This time he kept his arms loose at his sides, his
innards knotting up instead.

"You have to experience what it's like to be one of
my patients."

He thumbed through his mental schedule. "If you'll
give me a specific time, I'll see if I can make it out to
observe—"

"Oh, no. I don't mean you can watch. I want you

to 'do.'" She leaned a curvy hip against the rail of the wooden fence next to her.

"Do?" The muscles of his chest tightened, and he realized he'd crossed his arms again. This time he let them stay put.

"I want you to go through therapy as if you were one of my patients."

"I don't understand." Actually, he did understand. He just didn't want to. Already the gears in his head were beginning to whine like one of the bone saws he used in surgery.

Her smile grew, a genuine flashing of straight white teeth, her ponytail whisking back and forth as she shook her head. "You don't have to understand, Dr. Dunning. Not yet. You just have to show up."

CHAPTER TWO

SHOW ME YOURS, and I'll show you mine.

Trisha mounted and gathered the reins in her left hand, giving Brutus a quick pat on the neck with the other hand for standing still.

The good doctor had taken up her challenge two days ago and upped the ante in a way that was juvenile and yet, oh, so effective. He'd expected her to balk. Had counted on it, if she wasn't mistaken. She'd made a quip about how safe her horses were, that her patients hadn't shed a drop of blood yet—a good thing, she'd said laughingly, since she couldn't stand the sight of blood.

He'd gotten this speculative gleam in his eye as soon as the words had passed between her lips, then had issued his ultimatum. And assured her that his profession did indeed involve blood.

Was she game?

Game? Really?

She'd been forced to stab a man—had almost killed him. So the doctor's jibe had stuck in her craw. As if she had been some sissy, shying away from a paper cut or a bloody nose. It was so much more than that.

So she'd tilted her chin, taken her aversion to blood and guts and forced it to the back of her mind, drawing the heavy drapes closed on reality and agreeing to his request. He would sit through three sessions of therapy—as in literally sitting on Crow, her gentle giant—once he'd observed three sessions with a patient. She, in turn, had to sit in the glassed-in room above the surgical suite and watch him saw through a person's skull. That wasn't exactly the way he'd put it, but it was basically the same thing.

Dr. Dunning had definitely gotten the better end of that deal. Only she could tell that he didn't see it that way. His fear of Brutus had been almost palpable.

I was trying not *to scare him.*

That thought had never crossed her mind as she'd stood in that stall, her own knees quivering with terror when he'd silently motioned her out of there. He'd been as scared as she had.

Did that mean their mutual fears canceled each other out?

Hardly.

But if he could push through his, then she needed to try to push through hers. As it was, she'd seized his words, telling him that meant he had to "see hers' first—in other words, he was going to see how *she* operated. Whether or not he'd show up for her session with Bethany Williams this afternoon was still to be seen. She was counting on him really wanting to do what was right for his patient. And since Clara's team of doctors had done almost all they could for her through surgery and the normal course of physical therapy, her mom wanted to expand their horizons. Try some other options.

Trisha had only been in Dusty Hills six months, so getting the endorsement of a local neurosurgeon seemed a good way to get her name out…to put her on the path toward making it in this small town. If he could just see Clara on a therapy horse, he'd see how much it could help her. The five-year-old had definitely responded to the way Trisha had stroked her tiny fingers over Crow's inky-black coat. Trisha just needed Dr. Dunning to sign off on treatment, both for the sake of health insurance and her own liability insurance. Which reminded her, she'd have to list the good doctor as one of her patients for a little while so he'd be covered. Just in case.

She sighed and fanned her legs, making a clucking sound as she asked Brutus to break into a slow jog. She'd already warmed him up with some circles on the longe line, so he responded to the request quickly. "Someday soon I'm going to ask you to lope, big boy. Just to show you it's safe."

Her horse had endured the wrong end of a whip in his past life, the long pale scars—devoid of hair—visible on his haunches. He still shied away from sudden movements near his head—especially if those movements were made by a man—and Trisha couldn't blame him. He was as much in need of therapy as any of her other patients. So when she'd told Dr. Dunning he was a special case, she hadn't been kidding. But the horse had come a long way over the past several months. So had she.

In his own way, Brutus was helping her recover as much as she was helping him. Guiding the gelding to the center of the indoor arena to go through a large sweeping figure eight, they changed direction from clockwise to counterclockwise, and she smiled when one of his ears swiveled back to face her, listening for any verbal cues she might give. "Good boy."

Although Brutus had shown his nerves at Dr. Dunning's presence in no uncertain terms, things could have been a whole lot worse, according to what she'd been told by the rescue organization. Trisha might have maintained her poker face a little better than her horse had, but she hadn't been unaffected. Oh, no. Especially not once she'd realized the man had not been a killer sent to deliver a personalized anniversary message, courtesy of her ex-husband. Her fear had morphed into something else entirely when he'd flipped her onto her back, his firm warm chest pressing against her breasts, his breath mingling with hers. Her thoughts had taken off in other directions. Dangerous directions.

She'd wanted to wheel away from him just like her horse had. Only she hadn't been able to, and not just because he'd had her pinned to the ground with his body, hands imprisoning hers.

Two days later she still couldn't shy away from him. No, in all likelihood, she was going to have to work with the good doctor on a regular basis. *If* she could convince him she and her horses were not a danger to him or his patients.

To do that, she was going to have to find a way to keep her job at the forefront of her mind. And since he was due at the barn in two short hours, fifteen minutes ahead of her first young patient, she would have just enough time after working Brutus to shower and dress in something a bit more professional than her standard faded jeans and halter top combo. And somehow she needed to squash her silly reaction to the surgeon's presence. Especially since she had big plans for the man. Plans that included making him shed that thick coat of control he wrapped around himself and get him to agree that she could help some of his patients.

If she could just get the man to co-operate.

Hippotherapist does sound a little bit like hypnotherapist.

Mike turned his car into the driveway leading up to

Patricia's place. This could have all turned out differently had he heard Doris Trimble correctly. He'd been so sure she'd said she wanted her young daughter to visit a hypnotherapist that he hadn't even glanced up from his prescription pad, but had continued writing as he'd asked her what she thought that would accomplish. Then the word "horse' had been mentioned and his head had jerked up to attention as she'd explained about the new equine therapist in town. By the time he'd got the gist of what she'd been talking about, he'd been in too deep. He hadn't been able to just shoot the suggestion down, especially after getting a good look at the hope imprinted on her face. Clara had grinned wider than he'd ever seen as her mother had continued to make her case.

"Have you already taken her to see this person?"

"Just for a quick peek at the horses," she'd said, a fleeting look of guilt flashing through her eyes. "Clara seemed to love them. She responded immediately."

Perfect. This wasn't going to be a passing idea, evidently. He was either going to have to get behind the plan and support her, or give her at least one good reason why she shouldn't let Clara anywhere near Ms. Bolton or her horses. Hopefully that reason would come today.

There was no paved parking area near the barn, so he pulled into the same spot he'd parked in the last time. Glancing to his left, he spotted two horses close to the fence. They seemed to be studying his arrival with interest. He thought one of them might be the infamous Brutus. He could swear the animal on the right gave him a look of pure dislike, lifting his head to follow Mike's movements as he got out of the car. He had to fight not to climb back into his vehicle and beat a hasty retreat.

"Well, guess what? The feeling's mutual." He tossed

the words at the animal, only to stiffen when a quiet feminine voice answered him.

"What feeling is that?"

He swiveled around. Patricia Bolton had evidently come out of the barn when she'd heard his car drive up. He shrugged. "Just talking to myself."

She glanced out at the pasture, where Brutus was still staring at them. "I see."

"Ms. Bolton, look, maybe we can save ourselves both a whole lot of—"

She held up a hand to stop him. "Call me Trisha. My patients do."

His patients called him Dr. Mike, but it seemed a little presumptuous to ask her to do the same. So he said, "Okay...Trisha. Why don't you call me Mike?"

"Great. If you'll come with me, I'll show you how I prepare for my first clients of the day."

So much for leaving. She'd smoothly intercepted any pre-emptive strike he might have made and disarmed him.

Following her inside the barn to the very place he'd lain with her on the ground, the image of tangled arms and legs and of fingers running up his thighs came back with frightening clarity. He swore he could still feel her touch. He shook his head to banish the sensation.

There was a horse tethered in the same position that Brutus had been the other day, only this time there was some sort of saddle draped over a post, along with a brightly patterned blanket. "I was just grooming him before saddling up. This is Crow."

Pitch black without the slightest trace of white, the animal's coat had a healthy gleam that made Mike think she'd gussied him up just to show him off. His mane was even braided. She needn't have bothered, though.

Because just standing there near the horse made his gut contract.

"Do you want to touch him?" Trisha walked right over to the animal and stroked a hand down his neck, smoothing a misplaced braid.

"That's okay." He kept to the far side of the aisle, hoping against hope there wasn't going to be another incident like the one a couple of days ago.

"Come on. He won't hurt you. You've agreed to ride him next week, so you might as well get some of the preliminaries out of the way."

What had he been thinking, coming out here again? His wife had died handling one of these animals. Did he really want to do this? No. But something about Trisha's quiet voice and calm manner made him take a step closer. She wasn't afraid at all.

But, then, Marcy hadn't been either. And yet in the blink of an eye she'd been gone. And he'd still had to deal with her horses and clients in the midst of everything else. Thankfully, one of her close friends had helped out, going as far as buying the horse that had turned his world upside down. He'd tried to warn her off, but Gloria had insisted it was what Marcy would have wanted, that what had happened had been a tragic accident and not the horse's fault. She was probably right.

Still, he didn't want to be trapped in a confined space with one. Anything could happen. "Okay, but could we do this outside the barn?"

She blinked, but nodded. "Sure. Let me just saddle him up."

Making short work of it, she talked him through the process of swapping the animal's halter for a bridle, and then she explained the parts of the therapy saddle and showed him how to put it and the blanket on and how to tighten the strap beneath the horse's belly. Why she thought he needed to know any of this, he had no idea. Marcy had taken him at his word when he'd said he wasn't interested in riding. She'd never tried to force the issue. Maybe partly to cover up what she'd really been doing at the barn.

If he'd been with her that last day, would she still be alive?

That was something he really didn't want to think about too closely.

She gave the saddle one last check then said, "Okay, let's lead him outside."

His lips quirked. "No wheelbarrow today?"

"Nope." She grinned back at him. "You lucked out."

He wasn't sure he'd consider this lucking out, but he'd do whatever it took to get through this and head back to his own job. Where he felt secure and confident.

Like the last time he'd been here, he remained at Trisha's side as she told him that a horse should always be led from the left. "Have you ever been around horses at all?"

How to explain without...explaining? "I have, but I haven't worked with them closely."

There. Not bad.

Then she arrived at a rectangular fenced-in area that was covered with sandy-looking material. It appeared to have been freshly raked, a system of grooves running through the grains—for his benefit? She stopped and tied the reins to the middle fence post and glanced at her watch. "We still have about five minutes before Bethany arrives so why don't you introduce yourself to him? Come stand next to me."

Mike stiffened when she patted the animal on the neck. It was either explain why he had an aversion to horses or do as she asked. He moved closer as she continued stroking the animal.

"This is how I'd approach a patient who's here for the first time." She took Mike by the hand, her fingers firm against his as she lifted it and pressed his palm to the animal's coat, slowly guiding it down the length of the neck. "Isn't he smooth?"

Was he supposed to answer her? Because, no, it didn't feel smooth. All he could think about was how anything could happen. In the time it took for him to blink. And that familiar horsy smell that had clung to Marcy whenever she'd come home from the barn... It was right here, with all its terrible reminders of secret meetings and half-truths.

None of it was comforting.

And yet as Trisha continued to guide his hand in slow sweeping strokes over Crow's coat, the horse stood extremely still, as if he somehow sensed the turmoil lurking just below the surface. And slowly the textures and temperature of the animal's body began to make themselves known.

"Relax," she murmured, her voice like the softest silk. "He won't hurt you."

He couldn't bring himself to let his muscles go loose, but he did try to concentrate on things other than how huge and powerful the animal was. Like the warm grip of Trisha's hand as she held his. Like the scent of her hair and the tickle of her ponytail as it brushed his neck when she twisted her head. He concentrated on her instead of the horse. She bent a little lower, her hand guiding his down the upper portion of the horse's leg. "Crow could stand here all day and let you do this. He loves it."

He gulped. Crow wasn't the only one who could stand there all day. He was suddenly enjoying Trisha's touch a little too much, allowing his hand to rest in hers a little too heavily.

He didn't understand why his thoughts were even heading in this direction. He'd been with a couple of other woman since his wife's death, but those had been quick clinical sessions born out of physical need more than anything.

When Trisha's thumb curled into his palm as she lifted his arm to place it high on the horse's back, the friction caused a chain reaction in his body.

She wasn't purposely trying to switch on his motor, but it was cranking to life anyway. He tried to close his eyes to blot out her face, but it just heightened all of his other senses. The heat of her body next to his. The soothing little sounds she made as she murmured to the horse...to him.

"Isn't this nice?" she whispered.

Definitely not soothing.

"Trisha..." He turned his head to find her looking right at him, eyes soft and inviting.

He swallowed again.

Hell. He couldn't believe what he was thinking of doing. Or, worse, that he might actually be getting ready to...

His free hand came up to cup the back of her head, just as a shrill childish voice sounded from behind them.

"Cwow! Cwow! I come see you!"

Crow's head went up, and Trisha's eyes jerked away from Mike's, breaking the spell. She let go of him, and he took a couple of quick steps back, though she seemed to recover her composure with ease.

"Bethany," she said. "Hello! We've gotten Crow all ready for you."

A dark-haired child in a wheelchair rolled toward

them, accompanied by two women, one about Trisha's age and the other about twenty years older. The younger one came over and stood next to the horse, draping an arm over his neck as Trisha walked over to the other two. She embraced the woman and murmured something to her, then knelt in front of the child. "Are you ready for your ride? We're going to work really hard on our balance today, aren't we?"

The child nodded, her hands gripping the armrest of her chair as if she was preparing to rise. When she didn't actually leave the seat, Mike started to move forward to help, only to have Trisha meet his glance with a subtle shake of her head. He stopped in his tracks.

"Dr. Dunning, this is Bethany Williams and her mom, Gretchen. And this is my assistant, Penny."

He somehow managed to mutter out the appropriate greetings, although he was still feeling shakier than he cared to admit by what had happened a moment ago. He'd been about to kiss the woman.

Struggling to make sense of this crazy day, he watched while Trisha strapped a shiny black helmet onto the girl's head before helping her from her chair and leading her step by step to the horse. He was surprised by the headgear, but maybe things were different with kids. Marcy had certainly never used a helmet. If she had…

Mike turned his attention back to the girl to distract himself. She had a lisp, but her eyes were bright with intelligence. Her gait, though, was uneven and periodic shudders rippled through her muscles. Cerebral palsy? Possibly. She had enough control over her body that she could lift her foot toward the low stirrup with help and then between the three of them—helper on one side, Trisha and the mother on the other—they boosted her thin frame into the saddle. She immediately reached for and gripped the nylon straps on either side of the saddle for all she was worth.

She wasn't totally steady, but she wasn't afraid. Of that Mike was certain. Giddy was the term that came to mind. Once Bethany was in position, she grinned and scrubbed at the horse's shoulder with the tips of her fingers, still holding onto the straps. Her obvious joy at being there made Mike feel a little bit ridiculous about how cautious he'd been when even petting Crow. Then again, no one else had seen Brutus flip out a few days ago. And no one else had driven out to a barn four years ago to see why their wife wasn't answering his calls, only to discover her sprawled unconscious on the ground, a black horse that looked very much like this one standing over her.

But that's not what he was here for. Neither was he here to hit on the woman in charge of this horse and pony show. He was here to observe, and that's exactly what he should be doing.

"R-references?" Trisha somehow got the word past her paralyzed vocal cords, although she wasn't sure how. He'd watched her like a hawk the entire time she'd worked with Bethany. And out of the corner of her eyes she'd noticed him speak to the girl's mother. Gretchen loved bringing Bethany here. She figured of all her patients, Gretchen—a fellow horse owner—would be the most vocal about the benefits of hippotherapy. Which was why it shocked her so much to have him ask for references as soon as Bethany and her mom had left in their gray SUV.

"Yes. Mrs. Williams certainly seems to like what you do here, but I'd like to hear from a few people you no longer work with. Maybe a few clients from your last location."

So he knew she was fairly new to Dusty Hills but no way could she give him any names of people from her past. She stood next to his vehicle and thought through her possible responses. Why hadn't she realized someone could ask her this? Because everyone else had been happy to see her credentials—which were real enough. The FBI had somehow gotten them altered to show her current name, but all the classes and certifications were valid. They'd just cautioned her about using her university diplomas as actual references, or hanging any documents on the wall of her home or office, saying they wouldn't hold up if someone dug too deeply.

"I'd rather just stick with my current clients, if you don't mind."

His fingers paused on the door handle to his car. "Do you have something to hide, Ms. Bolton?"

Great, they were back to last names, evidently. She couldn't blame him but, dammit, she was good at her job—had worked hard to get her HPCS certification. Doing what she loved was the one thing that had been non-negotiable with her relocation deal, especially after everything that had happened. The only concession she'd made had been that she'd promised not to advertise or be listed on any specific hippotherapy database. Which meant word of mouth was all she had to go by—and it was proving much tougher than she'd thought in a small town like Dusty Hills.

She tried her rehearsed explanation. "I just think there are enough clients in the area, some of whom you probably know, who would be able to answer any questions you might have. I teach straight riding lessons as well. I can give you some of those names too."

He seemed to consider that for a moment or two before he relented. "I guess that will have to do, provided some of those names are from people who are no longer with you. I don't want there to be any question of conflict of interest."

Conflict of interest? She wasn't sure what he meant by that.

Did she have any patients she no longer treated? She didn't think so. Her client list wasn't that long, and those who were on it seemed to stick around. "Let me see what I can come up with, and I'll get back to you."

"I'm not a very patient man, Ms. Bolton. Don't make me wait too long." Mike opened the door to his car and propped one foot on the floorboard.

Don't make me wait too long.

A shiver went over her as her mind headed down a very different avenue. Had he said it that way on purpose? There was no indication he had, not even an embarrassed shifting of his glance away from hers. Just a cool, calm gaze that held hers far too long. How could the man wall off what had almost happened between them before Bethany's session? She was still a mass of conflicting nerves and emotions. Her legs were shaking, and she felt like she was going to lose it at any second. Mike, on the other hand, seemed to have forgotten…or maybe he hadn't been getting ready to kiss her at all.

That thought was even more mortifying. Could her radar be that far off base?

Evidently it could. At least, with this man.

Ha! Just look at how far off base she'd been with Roger, a man capable of murdering someone in cold blood and then acting as if *he* were the injured party. Even his name had been fake.

Yeah? Well, so was hers now. Evidently aliases were all the rage.

As Mike folded his length into his car and pulled out

of her lot in a cloud of dust, she gave a choked cough and noticed that Larry and Penny were both standing in the doorway of the barn, staring after the car. And Larry—the old coot—had the silliest grin imaginable on his grizzled face.

Oh, no. The last thing she needed was for them to get the wrong idea.

Because she was having enough trouble wrestling her own "ideas" back into place without giving them any more ammunition.

Ammunition.

Another shiver went through her, a little more wary this time as she remembered a few days ago—the way her fingers had clutched that hoof pick, palm sweaty, throat tight.

She'd thought she was going to die.

That's what she needed to focus on. What *could* happen, if she wasn't careful. What had already happened to the man who'd been sent to protect her a year ago. He'd died. All because of her.

Roger had almost killed her too, choking her on his desk in a jealous rage. Only her flailing hands had landed on a letter opener and she'd swung it round as hard as she could, stabbing him in the side. The FBI, alerted to the situation by their dying agent, had arrived in a hail of gunfire minutes later, arresting Roger and the rest of his minions.

Her ex had lived to stand trial, and he could still try to find her even now. He had the money and the contacts. The only thing she wasn't sure of at this point was how hot his rage still burned.

And how far those flames were able to reach.

CHAPTER THREE

"WE'RE WORKING ON IT. I want to observe a few more of Ms. Bolton's sessions before I'll feel okay recommending this particular course of treatment."

It was the best answer Mike could give Doris Trimble when she came into the office and asked again about going down the hippotherapy route. The woman nodded, the tightening of her hands in her lap showing she didn't really understand what the problem was, but she didn't try to pressure him into making a decision. She was willing to defer to his opinion, something that made his already low mood sink even lower.

He didn't want his personal history to get in the way of doing what was best for his patients. He just wasn't sure hippotherapy *was* what was best for Clara.

Then again, he was running out of options, other than saying that Clara's current condition was the best they could hope for: limited mobility and function. The swelling in her brain had subsided thanks to surgery and time, but the damage caused by the horrific car accident a year ago had not. She had burn scars on various parts of her body—the skin stretched tightly over the joints, making bending them difficult. Her mother seemed to think that riding would help stretch that skin and make it more supple. She was probably right about that. He'd watched how

Bethany Williams's body had moved with the horse and though it had been subtle, her limbs and joints had followed the animal's strides, her narrow shoulders stretching out and back as she'd gripped the straps on the saddle.

Muscle did have memory, so it was possible the same rhythmic movements could help Clara improve her balance and build some core strength. But improve cognitive function? That he wasn't sure of. He promised himself he'd take some time this week to do some deeper research.

It would have all been so simple if Trisha had landed in someone else's pond. But she hadn't. She'd wound up in Dusty Hill's tiny pool, and, as much as he didn't want to, he was going to have to make a decision on how to deal with her. Because even though he practiced neurology in the next town over, he had a feeling Clara's mom wasn't the only one who was going to discover Trisha's little outfit. More people were going to ask about her and her horses.

He knew exactly how much a referral from him could help her. He could be the best thing that ever happened to her, financially speaking. But that wasn't his main concern. He knew that sooner or later some of his other patients—whether they were past, present or future—were going to come into his office, eyes shining with excitement about the possibilities of hippotherapy, asking if it could help their relative. Could he prescribe it? He needed to have a ready answer—an objective one—one backed by research and unclouded by his personal issues.

He moved his attention back to the girl in the wheelchair. "Let's see how you're doing, Clara, is that okay?"

The lolling of her head was the only answer he got, as she struggled to focus on his face. Clara was seeing a variety of specialists today, her graft team, her occupational therapist, along with her physical therapist and orthopedist. They would come together later in the day and discuss their individual findings and try to figure out where to go from here. As he lifted Clara and laid her on the exam table, he wondered how Trisha expected to keep children like this upright on that horse. Crow—was that the animal's name?—was pretty large. He hadn't paid close attention to the sizes of the other horses. And that saddle had seemed soft and flimsy, with fabric grips rather than a traditional saddle horn. How would Clara even hold on?

He hadn't thought to ask, because something had distracted him. Namely the sight and scent of a certain equine therapist. One who'd stroked his hand down a horse's neck and made him wonder what it would be like to stroke his fingers down the silky skin of her throat instead.

"Okay, Clara." He reached over to grab his reflex hammer, putting Trisha out of his mind. "You know the drill."

She still couldn't sit completely under her own power, although he thought she'd grown a little more stable over the past few months. He smoothed a couple of strands of blonde hair back from her forehead with a smile that was a little more forced than normal. "Are you ready?"

He carefully went through Clara's reflex reactions and strength, looking for any increase in weakness or spasticity on her left side. Things looked much the same as they had a month ago, something her mother found frustrating, and Mike couldn't blame her. It had to be agonizing to work so hard and see so little improvement. It was another reason she was so eager to try something new. Anything new.

He couldn't let himself be swayed by that.

Helping the five-year-old back into a sitting position and calling her mother over to help keep her stable, he studied Clara's eyes, smiling at her and watching her re-action. Her lips curled as she tried to smile back, but the left side still lagged behind the right, not lifting as high. He did a few more tests and then they bundled her back into her chair and Mike gently strapped her in. Those blue angelic eyes followed his movements and he could almost see the plea inside of her, although he knew it was probably his imagination.

Shifting his attention back to Doris, he sighed. "Give me another week to get some more background infor-mation on hippotherapy. I'll give you a call as soon as I feel I can recommend something one way or the other."

Doris smiled, then, as if unable to resist, hugged him. "Thank you. I know you'll do the right thing." As soon as the words were out she released him and brushed her fingertips beneath her eyes. Mike's gut clenched. Again.

Doing what was right wasn't always a black-and-white decision.

He accompanied the pair out to the waiting room just as his receptionist swiveled in her chair. "A Ms. Bolton called to set up your next appointment. She said she's a hippotherapist?" Her puckered brow said she had no idea what that was.

Join the crowd.

Unfortunately, Clara knew exactly who that was. "H-h-h-horsy l-lady!" The stuttered words—the first thing she'd said since arriving—came out of the five-year-old's mouth as a loud squeal, causing every head in the waiting room to swivel toward them. So much for keeping Trisha's existence quiet for now.

Rather than feeling irritated, Mike squatted down in

front of the child and waited patiently until she looked at him. "Do you like the horsy lady, Clara?"

Clara's head gave that funny little roll that was meant as a nod. "N-nice. Want…h-horse."

"We'll have to see what we can do."

He glanced up at his receptionist. "Find a spot on my schedule that works for Ms. Bolton as well and pencil me in. Oh, and find my next scheduled tumor resection and ask Ms. Bolton if she can free up that time." If she was going to put his feet to the fire, then he intended to do the same. It was time for her to live up to her end of the bargain. And soon. He ignored the sharp twist inside him that said he wasn't being fair.

Of course he was. This was what they'd agreed on. Although, if he was honest with himself, he'd suggested the trade because of the way she'd shuddered at the word "blood" when she'd joked about her horses. He'd felt so sure she'd decide it wasn't worth it. That hadn't happened, making him wonder just how badly she needed new clients.

As he waved goodbye to Doris and Clara, a hard, cold lump formed in his throat. This was worst bargain he'd ever made. One that would require more delicate maneuvering than his most difficult surgery. And like most of those surgeries, the outcome was anything but sure. But first of all he wanted to see exactly *who* he was dealing with. There was something odd about Ms. Bolton…about the way she'd balked about giving him references from her previous location. He'd been lied to before. And unfortunately he'd found that some lies weren't harmless. Some of them destroyed lives.

Asking his receptionist for five minutes before sending in his next appointment, he made his way back into his office and dialed up an old friend. Swiveling away from the door, he waited through three rings then a familiar voice came on the line. "Mike. How are you?"

"Fine, Ray, and you?"

"Can't complain. Although things have been a little too quiet lately."

Mike took a deep breath before forcing himself to continue. "Well, maybe I can help you out with that. Can you do me a favor?"

The sheriff's gruff voice came back over the line. "Depends on what it is. Although I do owe you a pretty big favor."

"You don't owe me anything, Ray." His friend's mother had had an aortic aneurism, and Mike had steered them to the finest specialist in the area. The sheriff wouldn't let it go, saying he'd pay him back somehow.

"Sounds pretty serious."

It was. If only he could tell Ray why. It was a little hard as he wasn't sure of the answer to that question himself. "We have a new physical therapist in town who uses horses in her work."

"Oh, hell, Mike. Sorry, man."

His old friend knew all about Marcy. They'd all been friends once upon a time—had all grown up together in Dusty Hills. Ray even knew about the affair his wife had had with one of her fellow trainers. "It's not about her horses. I asked her for references, and she got a little squirrelly on me with her answers. Is there any way you can do a check on her?"

"I don't know, Mike. I'm assuming we're not talking about a credit check."

"No." He pushed ahead. He still had several patients to see so he needed to make this quick. "I have a patient's mother who wants to use her services, but I don't want to recommend something unless it's on the up and up."

"You think she has a record?"

Did he? No, not really, and he wasn't sure how ethical it was to ask his friend to do a background check.

"I'm not sure."

A chuckle came over the phone. "There is such a thing as the internet, you know."

Hmm…he hadn't thought of that. He typed the name Patricia Bolton into the computer on his desk and lots of suggestions came up. Too many. He wouldn't even know where to begin. "I guess I could try that."

"What's her name? I'll poke around some, but I can only dig so deep without having an iron-clad reason."

He swallowed, wondering if he was doing the right thing. This seemed a little too close to invasion of privacy for his taste. And just because Marcy had told some whoppers it didn't mean that every woman he ran across was stretching the truth. Except Trisha had definitely been evasive about giving him names of clients outside Dusty Hills.

We're talking about the welfare of a patient here.

Yes, they were. "I understand, Ray. Her name's Patricia Bolton."

"I remember her. Pretty little thing. She blew into town six months ago with a couple of men and an enormous horse trailer. The men didn't stick around more than a few hours. She, however, did."

A couple of men. That was strange. Ray or his deputy normally parked out on the main entrance to town, so it made sense that they'd see folks they didn't recognize every once in a while. Dusty Hills was a pretty close-knit community, most people lived and died in the same houses they'd grown up in, which was why his practice was in Mariston, a city many times larger than his hometown. "Maybe her husband travels or something," he mused.

The thought made a sick sensation worm its way through his gut. Especially after what had nearly happened between them—or maybe it had all been one-sided. He'd never thought to ask if she was married, although he hadn't noticed a wedding ring. Next time he saw her, he'd look a little closer.

"Maybe he does," Ray said. "I'll look in public records and see what comes up. If she has any outstanding warrants I'll let you know."

Mike scrubbed a hand across the back of his neck. He had no idea exactly what he was looking for. "Thanks. I have an appointment with her this Thursday."

"I'll give you a call on Wednesday, then. How's that?"

"Perfect."

"Oh, and, Mike?"

"Yeah?"

"You might not want to get too involved with her, just in case."

He could have set his old buddy's mind at ease about that possibility. Because he didn't plan to get involved with the woman at all.

What was he doing here?

Trisha's heart lurched as she glanced back and saw a familiar figure standing at the rail of her outdoor arena. Did he *enjoy* sneaking up on her?

It wasn't his fault that she was still jumpy this far after the trial. Or that being out of contact with her mother and brother had been weighing on her mind recently. She knew it was for their own protection, and she'd die if anything happened to either of them, but it didn't make it any easier. Watching her ex-husband gun down the man he'd accused her of sleeping with had driven home the dangers of getting too close to anyone. Roger might be in jail, but that didn't mean he didn't have friends on the outside.

Her eyes went back to the fence. She hadn't expected Mike to come to the barn until Thursday. But Monday morning found him with his forearms resting on the top rung, watching her as she coached her student over the first of the low jumps. Sweat trickled down her back—not just from the ninety-degree temperatures but in reaction to his unexpected presence. She tipped her wide-brimmed straw hat further back on her head, trying to slow her racing heart.

She'd had to supplement her hippotherapy income by giving riding lessons two days a week. This was one of those days. Mike hadn't called before coming, so she wasn't sure if he just wanted to talk to her or if he'd hoped to catch her with a patient. A kind of surprise inspection. Well, he'd surprised her all right.

She pulled her mind back to her student, calling out to her, "Don't forget to keep the reins loose as he goes over the cross rails. You need to support him but not restrict his head." She swiped at moisture on her temple with the back of her hand. "Go ahead and continue through the course."

The girl nodded her understanding and loped around the outside as she made her way toward the next jump.

Trisha glanced back at Mike, who now had a foot propped on the lowest rail of the arena. Still the same shiny uptight shoes he'd worn on his other visit. Very impractical for doing anything at her place. But maybe he'd come straight from work. If so, he was going to have to wait. She owed it to her student not to let her attention wander.

The next jump went without a hitch. Sarah sailed over the two-foot bar, letting her reins out and leaning low over the horse's neck as she went.

"Perfect! Good job. Head for the next one."

Keeping her eyes on her student, she edged toward the fence where Mike stood. At least Groucho, her gray lesson horse, was behaving perfectly. That had to be a mark in her favor.

She didn't turn her head, but once she reached him she murmured in a low voice, "Can I help you?"

He didn't say anything for a minute as if he was struggling with something. "Do you have those references I asked for?"

She blinked. He couldn't have called for that information?

"Sarah's—my student's—mom should be here in another ten minutes or so. Feel free to talk to her, if you'd like, although she's not one of my patients. The list of other references is in the house."

"You give lessons as well?" There was a harder edge to his voice that made her glance at him for a second.

There was that pulsing muscle again.

She focused back on Sarah's progress as she made it over another jump in the course and turned Groucho to head back to the starting position. "I'm fairly sure I mentioned that already. Until I have enough patients I'll need to keep the horses in shape and exercised." She shrugged. "Besides, I enjoy it. I'll probably continue even once my caseload expands."

Lord, she hoped it would. If only Mike would cooperate.

Sarah came level with them and drew to a stop, leaning over to stroke Groucho's neck.

"You did great, honey," Trisha said. "Why don't you walk him on the rail and let him cool down?"

"Okay, Ms. Bolton."

Trisha stiffened for a second then forced her muscles to relax. It still startled her to hear someone call her by that name, even after living with it for the last six months. At least the name Patricia was close enough to Patty Ann that she'd gotten used to it a little quicker. But Bolton was light years from the name Stoker, the name she'd been born with.

"You okay?"

Mike had evidently seen her reaction.

"I'm fine. It's just hot." As if to punctuate that statement, she swept the hat off her head and shoved her damp hair off her forehead, before replacing the headgear.

"Nevada can be pretty steamy. You're not originally from here?"

STS: short tenable statement. Something the agents had drilled into her head before they'd left her in a town so far removed from the bustle of New York City that she wondered if she'd ever get used to it.

"Nope. My dad was in the military, we traveled around a lot when I was a kid."

There. That had worked with most of the other people who'd asked about her past.

"Interesting. I've lived in the same spot my entire life. What places have you been to?"

Oh, Lord. At least Sarah was headed their way again, the interruption giving her a chance to think before she answered. She gave the girl a smile as she plodded by on Groucho. "You're doing great. One more pass and then you can take him back to the barn, okay?" Hopefully Sarah's mom would arrive and rescue her from having to remember the sequence of towns she was supposed to have lived in. They'd chosen places that were as far from her mother and brother's locations as you could get.

She quirked a brow, her legs feeling shakier than usual around him. "You want the whole boring list or just the highlights? I take it this is part of the job interview."

He smiled. "Sorry. Too nosy?"

Yes! And nosiness around the wrong people can be a very bad thing.

But she didn't say that. Instead, she shrugged. "Not at all. I just haven't lived a very exciting life."

Another lie. They just kept coming. But what choice did she have?

Mike leaned just a little bit closer, so close that she could feel his breath on her overheated neck. It felt cool and wonderful, drying some of the sticky perspiration. "I doubt that very much, Ms. Bolton."

The words made her glance at him sharply as Sarah continued around the track. She gulped. "Oh, I assure you it's true."

She put as much emphasis as she dared into the words, hoping it would derail him from asking her any more questions, then she looked back toward her student, who'd just dismounted and was leading Groucho to the gate. Trisha headed over to open it for her, relieved when Mike stayed put.

"Do you want me to put him up in his stall?" Sarah asked.

"How about if you rub him down and then let him out in the pasture. It's too hot for him to be confined." She didn't have any other students today. Besides, Groucho had earned a break for being such a good boy. She gave his neck a pat, smiling when he leaned over the fence and nudged her shoulder. "I think he agrees with me."

Trisha swung the gate open so Sarah could lead the

horse through. The teen unlatched her helmet and took it off, letting it dangle over her wrist. "Do you want me to send my mom out once she gets here? The girl's eyes skated to Mike, and Trisha wondered how much she'd heard of their conversation.

Mike wasn't paying attention to them, he was scribbling something inside the hard-backed notebook he'd brought out to the arena. Whatever. She still wasn't sure what he'd hoped to accomplish by coming out here today. "Why don't you have her pop out to say hi?"

"Okay." Sarah headed for the barn, Groucho in tow. Propping her hands on her hips and watching them move away from her, Trisha delayed having to interact with Mike again for as long as possible.

When she finally glanced back at him, his eyes were on the pair. "Don't you need to go with them?"

"Sarah's been around horses her whole life. She knows what she's doing. In fact, she and her mom are off to look at a horse tomorrow. She's ready to step it up another notch."

His mouth tightened, and she thought he was going to argue with her. Instead, he walked over and handed her a sheet of paper.

"What's this?" She looked down, trying to decipher his writing.

"A conditional recommendation for treatment. I did a little research over the weekend." He slid the clip on his pen onto the notebook's thin leather cover. "I can revoke it at any time, though. And I'll still want those references."

Despite the sliver of irritation that went through her at the imperious way he spoke of revoking his recommendation, it was soon dissolved by the rush of glee that swept over her. "You'll have them by tomorrow. Does this mean you're giving me the okay to work with Clara?"

He nodded. "I want to observe you with her, though, so if you could make the sessions for late afternoon, I'd appreciate it. If those go well, I'll consider sending a few other patients your way."

She wanted to wrap her arms around his neck and hug him tight…wanted to leap into the air and do a fist pump. But she forced herself to remain still and calm.

Be professional, Patty. Oops! Make that Trisha.

"Thank you, Mike. You won't regret it."

He gave a visible swallow. "Make sure I don't."

Sarah's mom came out, and Trisha introduced the two, tensing as she waited for Mike to interrogate her. But he didn't. He simply shook the woman's hand and asked how long Sarah had been taking lessons with her and how she liked it.

"My daughter loves Trisha. I don't think you could drag her away from this barn if you tried."

He nodded. "I'm glad she uses a helmet. It's important."

"Trisha insists on them. And I'm glad of it as well."

A glimmer of what might have been relief washed through Mike's eyes as he laid his arm along the top rail of the fence beside him. "Trisha seems to be a smart lady."

Did Mike believe that? Because she'd definitely gotten the idea that he didn't trust her or her horses. Maybe things were changing. A thought occurred to her. Maybe he would even reconsider making her watch him perform surgery. Yes! She'd been half-afraid it would bring back memories of Roger clutching his side, blood pouring from the stab wound and spewing words that had only half penetrated her brain. Until the Feds had broken in and taken charge of him. Trisha's fingers crept up to her neck as if she could still feel his squeezing grip. She straightened, dropping her hand when she noted everyone's eyes on her.

Sarah's mom smiled, breaking the awkward silence, and held her hand out to Mike. "It was nice meeting you." As they shook hands again, she said to Trisha, "We'll see you next week, then? Sarah wants to compete at the horse congress this year."

"She'll be ready. She's very good. And so is that horse she's getting. Thank you for letting me go out with you to look at him."

"She was thrilled. This has been her dream since she was a little girl, and I think she and Laredo will be a good match. She wants to train horses someday."

Mike's arm slipped off the rail, and his smile froze. Goodbyes were said, but the neurosurgeon was much stiffer than he'd been moments earlier. Why?

The man was impossible to decipher. She gripped the paper containing his recommendation a little tighter, half expecting him to wrench it from her hand and rip it to shreds.

As soon as Sarah's mom was gone, Trisha glanced up to find Mike's eyes on her. She wrapped her fingers around the warmth of the wooden rail to her right. "Did you want anything else?"

"I did, as a matter of fact. Did my receptionist call you?" His voice was soft, but there was still a thread of tension that ran through it.

"She did."

"The surgery is tomorrow afternoon. Can you make it?"

Her nose wrinkled. She'd so hoped he wouldn't make her go through with it. "What kind of surgery is it again?"

"I have to remove a tumor."

She swallowed. "But you've already agreed that I can help Clara."

"No. I've agreed that you can *treat* Clara. Under my supervision."

"You know nothing about horses."

His arms folded across his chest in a way that was becoming far too familiar. "You'd be surprised."

Surprised. How? "I thought you said you'd never really interacted with them."

"Let's just say I've seen more than I wanted to see."

Which told her exactly nothing. And far too much. Maybe she needed to ask for some references of her own.

"So you're going to let me supervise your patients and dole out advice to them as well?" As if she could remain upright long enough to watch him make his first incision. She'd probably pass out cold on the floor.

"That would be hard to do from your vantage point. You'll be in the observation suite above the operating room, remember?" Maybe the tension in her stomach came through in her face because he studied her for a minute, his own features softening. "If you want to skip the surgery, you can. We can meet in my office once I'm done and talk about your treatment methods. You can give me your references then."

She shook her head. "We had a bargain, and I'd like to stick to it."

Maybe she was crazy, but knowing the treatment area was in a separate room helped. She could close her eyes the whole time and block out what was going on below her. She relaxed a fraction. "So what time tomorrow? I have a lesson at one."

"Surgery is scheduled for four. If you're sure."

"I'll be there."

She reached up to adjust her hat, only to have him catch her hand and look at it, then slide his thumb over her ring. The act made her swallow. "What are you doing?"

"Do you always wear this?"

Licking her lips, she glanced down at where his thumb still fiddled with the fake class ring. Its purpose was to cover the pale patch of skin where her wide gold wedding band had once rested. Another suggestion from the Feds.

"Yes. Why?"

"Just wondered how safe it is for someone like you."

Her heart lurched. "S-someone like me?"

"Working with horses." He released her hand, and she let it drop to her side. "Couldn't it get caught on something?"

Oh, Lord, she needed to get a grip. "I'm careful."

At least she was trying to be, which was why she'd worn the ring in the first place.

He seemed to accept her words at face value because he went back to the previous subject. "I'll have my secretary call you with directions to the hospital. If you could get there a half hour early, that would be great. Things get hectic as it gets close to surgery time."

"I'll be there. And I'll bring the references." She wasn't sure how much longer she could keep putting it off.

Once they'd said their goodbyes and he'd left, Trisha fired up her computer to enter a reminder onto her calendar. And as her fingers hovered over the keys, she found herself typing in the good doctor's name...looking for what, she wasn't sure.

Nothing. There were a ton of Mike Dunnings in the world evidently. She narrowed the search, typing the word "Doctor' in front of his name and listing his location as Dusty Hills, Nevada.

There. A whole screen of possibilities.

Hmm…he had his own website. Interesting. She scrolled further down the list of results and found his name listed as Head of Neurology at a hospital in Mariston. And he was on various committees in Dusty Hills.

The tenth entry down made her pause, her brows coming together when she saw a picture of Mike with a woman. The black and white shot was grainy, but the couple were looking at each other and smiling. Then she looked at the title. Her eyes widened as shock rolled through her system.

She stared at it, unable to look away.

Oh, God. It explained everything. His reaction when Brutus had shied during their first meeting. His comment about not wanting to scare the horse. His dragging her bodily from the stall.

Not only had Mike been married. He had also been widowed. She read the headline one more time: *Wife of renowned local surgeon dead after tragic riding accident.*

CHAPTER FOUR

HE SHOULDN'T HAVE made her come.

He'd offered her an out at the barn yesterday, but he should have known she wouldn't take it. Mike pulled the overhead light above the operating table a little to the left to better illuminate the target area as he prepared to separate healthy tissue from diseased.

Trisha's green eyes had been feverishly bright when she'd met him in the waiting room an hour ago. At first he'd thought it was excitement, similar to what he felt each time he went into the operating room. Then he realized it was fear. Maybe even horror.

Like he felt whenever he was around horses?

Even after he'd realized she was scared, he'd still led her to the observation room. Like the ass that he was.

He could still remember touching that huge class ring on her finger yesterday and being far too glad it wasn't a simple gold band. Realistically, it would have been better if she wore a five-carat rock on that finger.

"Getting ready to dissect the tumor." He kept his voice calm as he spoke into the recorder, knowing she could hear every word he said, He may have been able to school his tone but, inside, his gut felt like a pile of scorched embers. Caused by regret?

Possibly. In fact, if he could stop the surgery right now

and send her home, he would. But he was too far in at this point. He wasn't going to risk his patient's life in order to ease Trisha's discomfort. He glanced up to the window to find her seated in the front row, her eyes closed tight.

Huh. Maybe she'd gone to sleep. Maybe he was worrying for nothing.

Somehow he doubted it. More likely she was avoiding looking down at where he was working.

His insides cooled just a bit. Okay, so she wasn't forcing herself to stare down at the surgery. That should help his guilt factor. Although it was still whispering that he should do something nice for her after this. Really nice.

Like what?

Using the precise laser and paying attention to the visual readout before him, he eased his way beneath the tumor, cauterizing blood vessels as he went. Millimeter by millimeter he began the delicate process of separation—one that would hopefully give his patient a new lease on life.

If only he could use the same process on his own life, cutting away all the heartache and betrayal and leaving behind only a good set of memories. Memories that were painless and fun.

Maybe even as much fun as he sensed he could have with Trisha, if he let himself go in that direction.

Not a possibility, unfortunately. Trisha might be perfect for some other guy, but not for him. An unwilling smile came up when he remembered her directing him to that wheelbarrow full of manure. Kind of fitting, really. He felt like his whole life had been wedged deep into a steaming pile of...

He shook his thoughts free and took a breath, his glance again skating to the window above him. This time Trisha's eyes were open and watching. The way she hunched lower in her seat told him he was wrong about her being okay with this. She wasn't.

You're not the only one who can read body language, lady. I bet you have no idea what yours is telling me right now.

Finishing the line he was making with the laser, he glanced at one of the nurses who stood at the ready in case he needed her. "Gail, I hate to ask, but would you mind going up to the observation room and telling Ms. Bolton she can go home? Tell her I'll call her later about our mutual patient."

The nurse's eyes went from his to the lone figure above them then she nodded, her brows not twitching an inch, although she had to be wondering why on earth there was a stranger in the deck above them. Everyone else was probably wondering the same thing, but no one dared ask.

"Do you want me to scrub back in afterward?" she asked.

"Yes, thank you."

Finally able to put Trisha out of his mind, he got back to the surgery, lifting out one part of the tumor and dropping it into a stainless-steel collection tray. "That needs to go down to Pathology. If they can look at it while I dissect the rest of the growth, I'd appreciate it."

"Right away, Doctor." His assistant quickly labeled the specimen and headed out the door with it.

Another four-centimeter segment of tumor to remove and then he'd re-examine the area and make sure he'd gotten as much as possible before closing up.

Less than ten minutes later Gail was beside him again, murmuring, "I told her, but she said she wants to stay until the end. She said she doesn't want to be the one to renege." The woman hesitated before finishing, "She said you'd know what she meant by that."

He did. Great. So much for making himself feel better. "That's fine. I just thought she might not be feeling well."

"Well…um, she did ask me to hand her a trash can." A chuckle accompanied the remark.

What? Surely Trisha wasn't seriously going to stay if she felt like throwing up.

If she did, that was her problem at this point. His was his patient.

Forcing his mind back to the procedure once and for all, he completed the surgery a half-hour later. The pathology results came back just as he was finishing up, so there was at least one piece of good news. The tumor was benign. It might slowly grow back after a year or two and have to be removed again, but at least it wouldn't spread to the far reaches of the patient's body and invade other cells. They could always try using radiation the next time to destroy the rogue cells, if its growth got out of control.

He reattached the section of skull he'd removed and stitched the edges of the patient's scalp together as neatly as possible. Her hair would cover everything once it grew back in. "Let's wake her up."

The anesthesiologist began lightening the sedation and removed the intubation tube as soon as the patient showed signs of stirring. Mike waited around until the woman could respond to simple questions, then gave her shoulder a gentle squeeze, promising to visit her once she got settled in the recovery area. He stripped his gloves with a frown and headed for the observation room, where Trisha—true to her word—still lingered. He pushed through the doors, his gaze stopping at the white plastic-lined can at her feet and finding it empty. Well, that was one less thing to worry about. He sat down beside her, aware that he was a little less composed than he would have liked. "You really didn't have to stay."

"I did. I didn't want there to be any questions later on."

Questions? She really thought he was petty enough to use that to prevent her from treating Clara? "You don't think much of me, do you?"

She studied his face for a few seconds. "Honestly? I don't know what to think of you. I feel like you're dismissing hippotherapy's benefits without knowing anything about it. It would help if I knew why."

Would it? If he told her what had happened to Marcy, would she feel better about his reluctance? Doubtful. She'd just give him the same line Marcy's friend had. *Accidents happen.* Yes, they did. But her friend didn't know the whole story about who his wife had been meeting that day. It had been Ray Chapman who'd gotten a visit from the mystery man a week after the accident—another horse trainer—who was supposedly as torn up by grief over Marcy's death as he was. She'd been planning on asking for a divorce. And he had never guessed. How much of a fool did that make him? His own wife had lied and cheated and he'd just kissed her goodnight at the end of each day without a care in the world.

He sighed and decided to evade Trisha's request. "I don't know enough about hippotherapy to make a judgment one way or the other. Which is why I thought this would a step in the right direction." He waved a hand at the room around him. "I thought we'd take a look at each other's professions."

Her brows went up. "Really? Is that what this was about? I thought it was about seeing who had the most guts." She swallowed, her glance going to the operating room below, which was being swabbed clean. "Okay, so that didn't come out exactly right."

He leaned back. "No matter. I'd say you were pretty gutsy for not walking away when given the chance."

"Don't worry. Your turn is coming. And don't expect me to give you an out when the time comes."

"So let's do it now."

Holy... Okay, so that had to be the guilt talking, because it sure wasn't him.

"Now?" She blinked.

"Why not?" He'd wanted to do something nice for her. How about putting his own courage to the test?

"I don't have any clients scheduled for today," she said, her voice thoughtful.

"Maybe we could jump ahead a bit and get this over with. You wanted me to see what it's like to go through a therapy session, right? Let's do it."

"You want to get on a horse." She sounded dubious. Almost as dubious as he felt.

"If that's what therapy involves, I'll get on one." *Clang, clang, clang!* The warning gong went off inside his head.

She sat up a little straighter. "You'd have to do exactly what I tell you, and Penny isn't scheduled to work today."

What did her helper have to do with anything? Unless maybe Trisha thought she needed a chaperone. After what had happened last time he'd been in her barn, maybe that wasn't such a bad idea.

"Thinking of feeling me up again?" He lifted a brow to show he was teasing.

Then his mind turned back to the task in hand and his smile instantly disappeared. "Are you planning on using Brutus?"

"With you? Oh, no."

"With who, then?" A chill ran over him. She said she

didn't use Brutus in therapy. Had she kept something from him?

Her head tilted. "Well, Penny's ridden him before. And, of course, I have. So has Larry. But I'd never let someone I didn't know ride him."

"Because of his issues."

She nodded. "Because of his issues…and theirs."

"Theirs"—meaning *his*? If that was the case, he was only too happy to be excluded from the hop-on-Brutus club. "As long as we're clear on this. You wouldn't use him with Clara. Ever."

"Not ever." Her voice was emphatic enough to convince him she meant it. "If you're serious about doing a session today, we probably need to get going before it gets too dark. I like to use the outdoor arena for my sessions rather than the indoor."

Interesting. He thought about asking why, then decided it might be better if he didn't know.

"Let me just speak to my patient and let my paging service know where I'll be."

"How about I meet you back at my place, then? I need to change and get a few things ready."

Change. Get a few things ready. A flashbulb went off in his head and illuminated a whole scene he shouldn't even be imagining. But he was. Things like glowing candles and skimpy nightwear.

"Great. I'll see you back there in an hour or so." With that, he stood and headed out the door. And away from those pictures of Trisha changing into something a little more comfortable—and a whole lot more dangerous.

"Hold onto the pommel until you get your balance."

Trisha frowned at the way Mike's knuckles grew white as he gripped the saddle horn and waited for her to set Crow in motion. Did he think she was going to start the horse out at a lope? She decided to set his mind at ease. "We're only going to do a slow walk."

"Right."

His voice was as tight as his grip. Something was wrong. No one should be this afraid. "I think we should call this off."

The man's head came up at that. "I thought you weren't going to give me a chance to back out."

"Changed my mind."

His jaw tightened. "Start him up."

That made her smile. "Sure, we'll just wind up that little crank on his side and he'll be ready for action."

His expression didn't budge. This man liked to be in control. She could only imagine how he must feel, letting someone else call the shots. Then again, maybe that's exactly what he needed. So if he wanted to go... they would go.

She raised the line attached to the horse's halter to get Crow's attention. "Okay, Crow, walk."

The horse knew this drill by heart. He carefully stepped out, not even the slightest hint of a lurch as he moved into a walk that was more of a glide. A show horse in his past life, he was the epitome of slow, methodical movements. Not even a swish of the tail disturbed the steady rhythm, nothing that could put a young, disabled rider off balance. "Good job."

Mike didn't say a word. He just held on.

Maybe it would have been better if they'd waited until Penny came in tomorrow—she could have walked beside him like she did with their other patients and act as a spotter—and an encourager.

"You okay, Mike?"

"Hanging in there."

"Don't worry. We won't go any faster than this."

His posture relaxed the slightest bit. Wow, for a neurosurgeon who performed operations on a regular basis he was really uptight. Then again, she knew why, and it made her heart ache. The news article said his wife had been found beside her horse—she'd died a few days later in the hospital, never having regained consciousness. Her organs had benefitted six different people. That hurt the worst. Trisha had a feeling Mike had been the one who'd had to make the decision no one should ever have to make: when to turn off the machines. She couldn't imagine anything worse. No wonder he held a grudge against anything equine. If she'd been in his place, would she be the same?

No, because she knew horses. Knew there was always a risk, just as there was with almost any activity. Riding a bike, paddling a canoe—getting married—nothing was completely safe. And she trusted her horses a whole lot more than she trusted most men nowadays.

But should she really be making him do this, now that she knew about his wife? If she insisted they not go through with it, though, he was bound to ask why. She doubted he'd appreciate knowing she'd looked him up online. So she let the horse do one complete circle around her and then reassessed his demeanor. Mike's form was actually not bad, except for that unyielding grip. Maybe she needed to do something about that.

"Remember, I'm controlling him with the longe line. You don't have to worry about steering him or keeping him at his current pace. Just concentrate on his rhythm. It's kind of a forward and back, push and pull motion. Feel it?"

His brows puckered as if he was concentrating, but

other than that nothing changed. "I'm not sure what I'm looking for."

"Close your eyes for a minute."

He shifted his attention back to her then did as she asked, his hands tightening their grip.

"Okay, concentrate on how Crow is making your body move. Because, even at a walk, his motions are acting on you, whether you're aware of it or not. Don't fight it. Let his strides carry you—really try to feel it in your hips. Keep them loose and let them move forward and back in the saddle." She waited for a second and watched his frame to see if he understood what she was looking for. She timed her voice to match each beat that the horse took, the slow gentle movements of Mike's body in the saddle. "Push. Pull. Hips. Moving. Forward. Back. Push. Pull. Slow. Rhythm. Don't. Rush."

Mike's eyes opened, his head turning toward her, some dark emotion coming from between the narrowed lids. "Believe me. I *never* rush."

Heat swept over her as his meaning hit her. Time to switch gears. "Crow, whoa." Right on cue, the large black horse slowed to a crawl and then stopped just as smoothly as he'd started. "Good boy."

Still looking at her, one of Mike's brows lifted.

"I was talking to the horse," she said, not sure what it was about him that made her mind stray into dangerous waters. "Why don't you give him a pat on the neck for doing what he was supposed to?" Maybe she should try to focus on her job, and remember who she was working with and why. Desensitize him. Show him that his wife's tragic death had been by far the exception to the rule…just like a plane crash. Or a boat accident. There were things in life that couldn't always be controlled.

Like marrying a man named Roger Smith whose real name had turned out to be Viktor Terenovsky—head of one of the most notorious Russian mafia groups? She'd pretty much felt completely out of control ever since that fateful visit from the FBI two years after her wedding. Things had spiraled out of control after that, when they'd planted an agent at the house. Six months later, the agent had been dead, her marriage had been annulled and she was in the witness protection program. And her husband—who'd vowed to hunt her down and make her pay—was in a federal prison for the rest of his natural life. But not before he'd ruined her life as well, effectively separating her from everyone she'd ever loved. Her throat clogged, wondering how her mother and brother were doing.

"Thank him?" Mike asked, bringing her attention back to him. "You mean like pet him?"

She drew a careful breath and tried to focus. "Yes. That's exactly what I mean."

He seemed to close his eyes for a second, as if trying to wrap his head around her request, before leaning forward and pressing his palm to Crow's neck then quickly removing it. "Would you make your clients do this?"

"Absolutely. Penny would probably have to help them, but it's important for my clients to realize these horses are living creatures who are an important part of their therapy team. They need to say thank you, just like they would thank a human being who helped them."

"So I just thanked him."

"You did." She wasn't sure exactly how much Mike was expecting her to do with him. "Are you up for another round?"

"How long do you normally work with your patients?"

She shifted the long length of longe line to her other hand. "A half-hour to an hour, depending on their abilities."

"And we've been working...?"

She smiled. "Oh...about five minutes, give or take a minute."

"Crap."

There was a wealth of meaning in that single word. "You ready to quit?"

"No. If you could make it through my surgery, I can make it through your treatment."

A flash of admiration went through her, and she wondered how far he was willing to let her go. How much control was he willing to relinquish? "How was your balance that last round?"

One side of his mouth quirked. "I didn't fall off, so I guess it was fine. Why?"

She'd thought it was pretty fine herself. "I'm thinking you might be ready to advance a step. Try something just a bit harder."

"You said we were only going to do this at a walk."

"Yes. And we are."

"So by harder you mean..."

Her lips curved. "Have you ever ridden a bicycle with no hands?"

"No hands? Are you kidding me?"

"Nope. Put your hands on your thighs and just sit there for a minute."

Mike's chest inflated as he took a deep breath and held it then released it. He took one hand off the pommel and rested it just above his knee. "You're not going to start him up again, are you?"

"No. I'll let you know before I do anything."

Off came the second hand, which went to his left

thigh. He sat there like an abandoned ventriloquist's puppet, not a single muscle moving.

She nodded her approval. "Good. Now put your hands back on the pommel."

Mike went back to his previous position, although his fingers weren't quite as white this time.

"Okay, we're going to walk again. Concentrate on your balance. When we come up on the halfway point, which will be at the far end of the arena, let go of the pommel one hand at a time, like you've just done, and grip your thighs. You'll still have the illusion of holding on, but your abs and leg muscles will be doing most of the work."

His frown returned. "And if he takes off?"

"He won't. Unless you kick him."

"No chance of that."

She lifted the longe line again to signal to Crow that he was going to move in a minute. "Just take it slow and easy. Ready?"

He nodded.

She gave the command, and the horse went back into his careful glide. Holding her breath, she could almost see the gears turning in Mike's brain as he tried to figure out if he was really going to do what she'd asked. Up came the halfway point and one hand came off the pommel. He stayed like that for a few beats then added the second hand.

"See if you can keep your hands there for ten strides. Count them. Out loud," she added, in case he wasn't sure.

"One…two…three…four…"

His numbers were more an afterthought than anything, because she could tell all his concentration was on keeping track of Crow's movements. Plod, plod, plod. Mike kept perfect pace with his counting, his hips moving back and forth. When he hit ten, he glanced at her in question.

"You can put your hands back on the pommel."

Once he did, she asked Crow to stop again. "Really, really good. Now thank him again."

She could have sworn his eyes gave a half-roll, but he did touch the gelding's neck again, holding the pressure for a little longer this time. "He doesn't act like he even cares."

"Oh, he cares." And so did she. She was feeling a combination of pride, elation and some other emotion she couldn't decipher. "I'm going to walk toward you. Stay in the saddle until I reach you. Then I'll tell you how to dismount."

The man actually chuckled in response.

She began looping the longe line around itself as she made her way toward the pair. "What?"

"I hadn't actually thought getting down might be a problem. Until now."

She smiled back. "We'll worry about that in a minute."

Once she reached him, she held onto Crow's halter. "Okay, reverse what you did to get up. Swing your right leg over Crow's back, then kick your left foot out of the stirrup and slide down his side...hopefully landing on your feet, if all goes well."

He followed her instructions, except as he started to slide down the horse's side, she stepped closer, reaching out with both hands to steady his descent, palms sliding up his sides. His breath hissed in at about the same time as hers whooshed out of her lungs at the contact. The second his feet touched the ground, he went very still.

Did he think she was feeling him up again?

This isn't one of your patients, Trish. She started to

let go and take a step back, only to have him grab her hands and keep them in place.

"Sorry," she said. "I'm used to working with kids who aren't very steady."

"Yeah, well, I'm feeling none too steady right now myself." Still holding one of her hands, he turned round to look at her, his back to the horse. He nodded at the longe line she still held. "Do you need to put him somewhere?"

The low tone made her blink. He was still gripping one of her hands, making no effort to let her go. The scent of soap and warm horse rose between them, teasing her nose and jarring her senses. The combination was earthy and real and, oh, so sexy. "I—I can unsaddle him in a minute. I'll just unclip him so he can go over and get some water."

He released her. Trisha's hands shook as she unsnapped the line from Crow's halter and let him go. The gelding headed straight for the far corner of the outside arena, where he could see the inside of the barn and the other horses who were still in their stalls.

Why had he wanted her to let Crow go? Because the horse made him nervous? Or for some other reason?

You're being ridiculous. He's probably going to chew you out for touching him again. Or maybe he just wants to co-ordinate our schedules so he can watch Clara's first session.

Maybe he hadn't even felt that amazing jolt of electricity that had passed through her as she'd touched him.

His hands went to her shoulders, and he turned her around to face him. The look in his eyes said she was very, very wrong. He'd felt it all right.

And he was about to do something about it.

CHAPTER FIVE

THIS WOMAN WAS going to be the death of him.

First she called out commands that sounded a little too close to an instructional sex video—raising disturbing images in his head. Such as what it would be like to do those things while horizontal, with a certain hippotherapist wedged beneath him. Only there'd be no "nice and easy" or "slow" about it. If they ever came together, it would be hot and intense and incredibly carnal.

Then she'd told him to grip his thighs and count out loud. More pictures had formed. Equally disturbing.

Her hands sliding up his sides as he'd gotten off the horse had added the final log to the fire—one he'd been doing his hardest to put out. It made him wonder if she'd done it all on purpose—although if she had, he had no idea why.

"Is there a problem?" Her wide green eyes held a trace of wariness along with a whole lot of something else.

"Are you *trying* to get something started here?" If she'd been attempting to rattle him, she'd done a fine job of it. He *was* rattled. And he only knew of two ways to fix the problem. One…run like hell. Or two…kiss her until he no longer cared.

Unfortunately, since he was in a sandy fenced-in arena, getting out quickly might prove a physical impossibility. Not to mention a certain part of his body was yelling for him to choose the second option, no matter what it might lead to.

"What do you mean?"

"I mean it's been a while, but I don't think my brain has completely forgotten what it's like when there's a certain amount of chemistry between two people."

"Chemistry?"

She'd injected a note of uncertainty into her voice, but the way she moistened her lips said she knew exactly what he was talking about.

"Are you saying you haven't felt a spark or two when we've been together?" Even during that first panicked meeting, something warm and molten had flowed between them.

"I don't know what you want me to say."

He took a step closer, his hands leaving her shoulders and cupping her cheeks, instead. "I don't *want* you to say anything, Trisha."

"Oh."

He couldn't hold back a smile. "Can you come up with one valid reason why I shouldn't do something incredibly stupid right now?" His thumbs strummed along her cheekbones, the skin soft and warm. "Think hard."

Her lips parted then her hands went to his forearms, sliding slowly up to his shoulders. "I'm drawing a blank."

"Hmm. Well, then, that makes two of us." He glanced to the side where the horse stood, head hung over the gate, before his arm went around her waist and reeled her in. "Think he'll stick to his side of the room?"

"Pretty sure he's not interested in anything we're doing right now."

"What about what we're *about* to do?"

With a pre-emptive "Hail Mary" or two that he hoped

would see him through, Mike lowered his head and covered her mouth with his.

Her lips were every bit as soft and moist as he'd feared. Or was it hoped?

It didn't matter, because the woman wasn't just letting him kiss her. She was kissing him back, her mouth sliding over his in perfect counterpoint to the movements of his. And when he opened, so did she, to the devastation of anything rational that was left inside him. His tongue immediately surged forward, affirming his earlier thoughts that this woman did not generate anything soft and gentle in him but rather an urgency he was suddenly having trouble reining in.

When he tried to draw back, however, Trisha was right there, making sure he didn't go far. She made a little sound in her throat when he went deeper, her fingertips pressing into the skin at the back of his neck as she leveraged him even closer.

One of his hands went to the small of her back, warning her that she was playing with fire. It backfired, though, because trapping his flesh between the taut muscles of her belly and his own pelvis was a pretty good imitation of something else. The tight space made him want to do one thing and one thing only: thrust forward hard and fast. He did the next best thing and lived vicariously through his tongue, allowing it to act out his fantasies in her mouth, his hands moving to cup that luscious behind he'd admired, keeping her hard against him.

Instead of letting him have his fun and pulling free before he got beyond the point of no return, though, her fingers went to his polo shirt and yanked it up from his waistband, allowing her access to his skin. Wasting no time, she burrowed beneath the opening and splayed her hands out on his bare back, her touch sending a jolt of need racing through his system.

He left her mouth, skimming across her jaw with biting kisses he vaguely worried might be a little too rough. Until she tilted her head toward him with a low moan that sounded almost as desperate as he felt. He took his cue from her and jerked her shirt from her jeans, continuing around her waist until it hung free. He didn't head for her back, though. With his lips pressed to her neck, his fingers skated up the smooth skin of her sides and found the curves he was looking for. Her warm breasts, encased in a satiny cocoon that squeezed them together. He moved his body sideways to give him more access, while maintaining enough pressure on his erection to keep it from raging at him in despair.

Taking a second or two to breathe, he slowly allowed his fingertips to drag over her bra, bumping softly over the tight nipple at the very center of the cup and then coming back to do that again. Trisha's throat moved against his lips as she swallowed and her back arched slightly, moving into his touch.

It was then that Mike had his first doubts about how far Trisha was willing to let this go. Or how far he was willing to take it. Mike had stopped carrying a condom in his wallet the day he'd said "I do" to Marcy at the altar. After her death he hadn't been able to bring himself to go back to those old habits.

Putting Trisha or anyone else at risk was not an option.

He somehow forced the muscles in his arm to obey his thoughts and pulled it free of her shirt. His head came up, and he found Trisha's eyes already open, staring at him in some confusion.

She wasn't the only one who was confused. He hadn't gotten this carried away since...well, in a long time. With that realization came the guilt. He couldn't even remember what it had been like to feel that for Marcy, although he knew he had at one time.

He eased his hips back, allowing the dull ache of withdrawal to pull him back to earth. Back to sanity.

She was still looking at him. To blot out that view, he pressed his forehead to hers. "I don't know what I was thinking. I'm sorry."

Trisha's hands came out from beneath his shirt as well, and he felt her shrug. "I don't think either one of us was doing a lot of thinking. No need to say you're sorry."

Like hell there wasn't. But he wasn't sure if he was apologizing to Trisha or to Marcy's memory. Either way, it wasn't something he wanted to analyze right now. "Right." He completed the separation process and took a step back. "I'll just go, then."

"Okay."

She tucked her hands into the back pockets of her jeans, her T-shirt still skewed sideways and perched high enough on her left side that he could see an inch or so of creamy white flesh. She made no effort to tug it down. Her posture showed off the tight peaks of her breasts still very much in evidence. She either didn't realize it, or she didn't care. He had a feeling it might be a little bit of both.

Marcy had always been so meticulous about the way she'd dressed, even on the days she'd gone out to the barn—of course, knowing what he did now, her reasons seemed pretty obvious. His glance went to the far side of the arena, where Crow stood, saddle still in place, looking bored by the whole scene. Trisha was right. The animal didn't care about what the two strange humans had been doing.

For the first time in his life he wished he could look inside a horse's mind and borrow a little of that couldn't-care-less attitude. Because right now he did care. As he stiffened his shoulders and swung away from woman and horse, heading for the open barn door on the side of the arena where his car was parked, he could still feel her looking at him. But she didn't say anything else or give any indication that she wanted him to stay.

That had to be a good thing, right? If ever there was a woman he should stay away from, it was Trisha.

He emerged from the barn and blinked at the sun a time or two before digging his car keys from his pocket and settling into the beige leather seat of his vehicle. Putting the car into drive, he headed down the long gravel driveway. The dust kicked up by the vehicle blotted out the view in his mirror. Another very good thing.

Because if he couldn't see it, he could pretend it didn't exist. Just like a child playing peek-a-boo who hid behind his hands. If he kept the idea firmly in his head, it would become true, sooner or later.

He had a feeling it would be later, however. As in a couple of decades from now.

"Looks like horses aren't the only things that scare him, Crow." Trisha stroked the horse's neck, leaning her forehead against him, only to pull away again when it reminded her of the way Mike had pressed his forehead against hers, his breathing still rough and uneven.

She shivered.

He'd run from the scene of the crime so fast that she'd barely had time to pull her thoughts back together, much less try to convince him to move to the nearest clean stall, which was where her thoughts had been centered the second his mouth had hit hers.

She'd been looking for release. That had to be what it was. Her body was still on high alert, even now, and it had been over thirty minutes since he'd left. If he came back, she couldn't guarantee she wouldn't melt right back into his arms.

Scratch that. She *would* melt into them.

She'd forced herself to go through the motions of unsaddling Crow and giving him a good rubdown. But her eyes and ears had been watching for any sign that Mike might have changed his mind. But once the roar of his engine had faded, it hadn't come back.

What was she doing, playing around with something as serious as this? She was supposed to be living a quiet, uneventful life, not getting involved with a man she barely knew. Wasn't that what had gotten her into trouble in the first place? Roger had wined and dined her so quickly she'd barely had time to catch her breath. The truth was, he'd been obsessed about having her, and once he had he hadn't wanted anyone else near her.

The solution? He'd married her.

But what she'd once thought was old-fashioned and sweet had soon turned into a nightmare from which there'd been no escape. In the end, he hadn't been "Roger" at all, but a cold-blooded killer. The funny thing was, she was now following in his footsteps. Not the killing part but the hiding-behind-a-fake-name thing. He'd gone by a false name at the beginning of their relationship, and now she was going by one at the end of it. How turned around things had gotten once the Feds had come and revealed the scope of her husband's ruthlessness. He'd controlled a whole lot of lives, including hers.

She swallowed. Did she really want to drag Mike into all that? Feeding him phony bits of information in an attempt to keep him in the dark? Wouldn't that make her the same as Roger?

Her ex had claimed he'd done it to protect her.

Well, she was doing exactly the same thing. Lying to protect people. Only she was doing it to protect their lives, not someone's fragile sensibilities.

Besides, Mike had been hurt once already—terribly. Could she risk being the cause of him getting hurt again?

He doesn't love you. He was only interested in a quick roll in the proverbial hay.

Well, that's all she'd been interested in as well. It would have been so easy to just do it and then go their separate ways. After all, it happened all the time in the real world. Have a few drinks: wind up in bed. Meet up in a chat room: head for the nearest motel. Give a man a riding lesson: have sex in a deserted barn.

Easy.

So why, then, had he run?

She scrubbed her fingertips behind one of the gelding's ears. "Be glad you don't have to worry about anything other than food and a warm place to sleep."

The horse's left ear swiveled in her direction and he blew out a breath, as if giving a sympathetic sigh for her trials. Or maybe he was just bored.

Laughing, she took hold of his halter and snapped a lead line onto it. "Let's put you with your buddies, okay? You can take the rest of the day off."

Trisha led him out of the arena and headed across the lot toward the pasture.

Sarah had called a few minutes ago, which was another sign that she and Mike stopping when they had was a good thing. Her student had been out to check on the horse she'd bought and asked if Trisha would come out and help trailer him for the trip home. So at least she wouldn't have to think about Mike or what had almost happened for a while. As of Thursday, though, he was scheduled to come out and watch Clara Trimble have her first physical therapy session.

No problem. She could and would face him without batting an eyelid. She had to. Somehow. She'd come down this road looking for a referral and she'd do whatever it took to get one. It would mean her new lifestyle would be safe without the Feds having to step back in and find her an alternate job, which was what they'd wanted to do in the first place. So if she could just get Mike to agree to endorse her...

Her mind slithered into uncomfortable territory as a memory of their time in the barn flooded back to her. Surely he wouldn't think she'd kissed him to have access to more of his patients. No, he'd already given her the okay to take Clara on as a client. But he might think she was hedging her bets for the future.

Maybe she should call him. And say what? *Hey, I wasn't going to have sex with you just to get my hands on your patient list—honest.* Wouldn't calling to deny a question that had never been asked amount to a confession? Or at the very least plant a seed of doubt in his mind?

Better to just act like nothing had happened.

She slid the latch to the pasture gate free and let Crow loose to graze for the rest of the afternoon. Acting like nothing had happened sounded like a good plan.

Now all she had to do was get her head and her heart to co-operate. Because right now they were still focused on her empty driveway and hoping against hope she might see that cream-colored car heading back her way.

CHAPTER SIX

MIKE WAS HALFWAY to his car after a long day at the hospital when his phone vibrated against his hip. He rolled his eyes. *Can't I get out of the parking lot first, guys?*

He'd already had a day from hell, his teeth clenching at the memories of yesterday's kiss until the muscles in his jaw ached from fatigue. Dumping his car keys back into his front pocket and grabbing his phone, he glanced at the readout.

He frowned. Not the hospital after all. It was a Dusty Hills number. Punching "Talk", he lifted the phone to his ear.

"Dunning here."

"Mike?" The low throaty voice was the one that had haunted him for the last twenty-four hours.

"Trisha? Is everything okay?" He couldn't imagine her calling him just for kicks. Besides, she sounded funny.

"No. They're bringing Sarah in. Are you at the hospital?"

"Sarah?" He racked his brain. The name was familiar but... Wait. "Is she the student I met?"

"Yes." There was the shrill sound of a siren on the other end of the phone. "We went to get her horse and..." She said something to someone in the background.

At the word "horse", icy needles had begun pricking

at his scalp in a thousand different spots. "Did something happen?"

"There's been an accident." A second or two of silence. "Are you at the hospital?"

An accident. Dammit! He reversed course. "I'm here. How far out are they?"

"Probably fifteen minutes. Her mom is in the ambulance with her." Trisha's voice was so shaky he could barely make out the words. "I need to go. I have to take care of the horse. Call me when you know something."

His jaw clenched again, his aching muscles protesting the action. "Stay away from that horse, Trisha."

"What? No, I can't. I have to help. I'll call you later." With that the line went dead.

Crap! He strode through the hospital doors, already hitting the redial button of his phone. It rang four times on the other end, and then Trisha's voice mail picked up—her pre-recorded voice sounding obscenely cheerful. A million words—none of them good—went through his head. He didn't even know where she was. Was she at her place? All Mike could picture was that huge horse she'd been grooming the first day they'd met. Had he—or Sarah's new horse—gone crazy somehow?

Getting involved with Trisha in any way, shape or form had been a mistake. As soon as he had finished assessing Sarah, he was going to call Clara's mother and tell her he was revoking his recommendation. If Trisha was boarding unsafe animals, he didn't want his patients anywhere near that place. Although, if something happened to her, it was a moot point.

He swallowed hard as he arrived at the emergency room to find Peyton Wright, one of the ER doctors, on the phone. He motioned to Mike, covering the phone with one hand. "I was just about to page you. We have a head trauma coming in."

The chilly sensation of déjà vu slithered through Mike's gut and coiled around his spine. He shut down that line of thought as soon as it started.

"Teenage girl?" he asked, even as he hoped it was someone other than Sarah.

Peyton's brows went up. "Yep, I'm on with the ambulance right now." He finished giving instructions to the emergency services crew then got off the phone. "Looks like we've got a possible concussion or skull fracture, along with a broken femur.

The horse had thrown her? "Riding accident?"

"No. Car." He paused. "Are we talking about the same case?"

Trisha had said there was a horse involved. "Do you have a name?"

"A Sarah Millner?"

Mike nodded. "You sure the injuries are from a vehicle?"

"That's what they said. The other driver was drunk. He's coming in too, but doesn't seem to be injured. He'll be headed for jail as soon as he's been assessed, from what I understand."

Maybe he'd misunderstood her. Maybe she wasn't at the scene of the accident. Maybe Sarah's mother had called her and told her. His jaw loosened fractionally. That had to be it. Her voice had been shaky so whispers from his past had hijacked his imagination, playing tricks on him.

The ambulance pulled into the bay just a few minutes later, and Mike's concentration went to his patient. As the paramedics wheeled her in, rattling off vitals and their findings in the field, the familiar blonde hair and ponytail told him it was indeed Trisha's student. Her mother ran alongside the gurney. Peyton took the lead, while Mike tried to piece together what had happened. "They said it was a car accident?"

The frantic woman dashed the back of her hand across her eyes. "Yes, we were hauling her new horse home and someone ran a red light and hit Sarah's side of the car. The police say he was drunk." Her voice dropped to a whisper. "The airbags went off, but once I realized what had happened and turned to her, her side of the car was pushed toward me, and Sarah looked…" Her voice gave way. "She looked like a broken doll."

"We're going to do all we can for her." He motioned to the nurse. "She needs to get some information from you. Is Sarah allergic to anything?"

"Codeine makes her vomit, but other than that, no." The gurney made a quick turn, leaving them behind. "I want to go with her."

"You can in just a little while. Let us check her over first, okay?" He squeezed her shoulder. "I promise I'll come out and find you as soon as I know something." A random thought went through his mind. "Was her instructor in the car with you?"

When the woman looked confused, he tried again. "Was Trisha—Ms. Bolton—there?"

"She was following us in her car." Sarah's mother looked at him a little closer. "You were at her barn the other day, right? You asked me some questions."

He nodded, knowing he needed to get back to where Sarah was but also knowing that Peyton wouldn't hesitate to haul him back there if he needed him. "That's right. Was Trisha involved in the accident?"

Her eyes filled again. "No. Oh, God, Sarah's poor horse. She'll never forgive me if he doesn't make it. The trailer tipped over during the accident and…Laredo was thrashing and screaming. I could hear him banging against the sides of the trailer, but I had to take care of Sarah. Trisha offered to stay and help get him out."

"Of course you had to take care of your daughter." He replayed Trisha's words in his head and his gut tightened into a hard ball. She was there. At the scene. Trying to take care of an injured and frantic animal. That's why she hadn't answered his call. "I'll go and check on Sarah."

He strode down the hallway, pressing the redial button on his phone as he went. Again, it went to voice mail after a few rings. Mike had visions of Trisha injured or worse as she tried to deal with Sarah's horse. There was nothing he could do about it right now, though, he already had one patient. All he could do was pray it wouldn't soon be two.

"How is she?" Peyton was bent over Sarah, examining her.

"Pulse is strong and regular. Pupils look good. The EMTs called it: her femur is broken and it looks like she's got a concussion, judging from the contusion on her forehead." He took a step back. "You want to take a look?"

Mike examined her, paying special attention to her skull. No depressions that he could see, although she did have a huge purple knot forming where the left side of her forehead had hit something hard. "I want a CT before anything is done to her leg, just to be safe."

"You want to order it?"

He wanted to go to Trisha, but his place was here. For now, at least. "Yep." He marked her chart and made the call, going with her to the imaging area. Fifteen minutes later they had their answer. She did have a concussion, but she was already regaining consciousness. Mike accompanied her to her room, where Peyton would see about her leg, and then headed for the waiting room. Her mother had to be frantic.

As soon as she saw him she stood slowly from her chair, the terror in her eyes obvious. He flashed a quick thumbs-up sign just to put her at ease, and she sagged back into her chair, tears running down her cheeks.

"She's got a concussion and her left leg is broken, but she should be fine. They're getting her settled in, and once they do, you can go back to see her, okay?"

"Oh, my God. I was so scared. She wasn't moving, wouldn't answer me." She pushed back a strand of hair with a shaking hand. "Thank you so much."

"You're very welcome. I'll be available if you need me." He jotted down his cellphone number on the back of a business card. "Call me if you have any questions. We'll want to keep her tonight, but I think she'll be able to go home in a day or two. Nothing strenuous until that leg heals."

She nodded. "I'll make sure she rests."

"Any news on her horse?"

"Nothing. Trisha said she'd call as soon as she could."

Those pricking needles went back to work on his scalp. "Where did the accident happen?"

"On Santa Fe Road, near the big water tower."

He knew where that was. His fingers closed around his cellphone. The smart thing would be to simply try to call her again, but that's not what he wanted to do. "I'm sure they're doing all they can for…Laredo, did you say his name was?"

"Yes. I hope you're right. I don't know what I'm going to tell Sarah if she asks."

"Just tell her he's being taken care of. No need to panic her just yet."

One of the nurses appeared in the doorway. "Mrs. Millner, I can take you to see your daughter now, if you'd like."

"Yes." Sarah's mom picked up her purse and headed after the nurse, stopping for a second to thank Mike again.

As soon as she was around the corner, he knew what he was going to do: head for Santa Fe Road.

Trisha pulled her knees up to her chest as she sat on the floor of the empty horse trailer. Where the hell was that tow truck anyway? A police car still sat off to the side, the officer writing up his notes. She could probably leave the scene and let the police take care of it, but she'd promised Sarah's mom she'd stay here.

Now that Laredo was safe and in good hands, she wanted to be at the hospital, making sure Sarah was okay. Every muscle in her body ached from trying to get to the injured horse and free him from the overturned vehicle. They'd ended up having to winch the trailer back into an upright position in order to free him and coax him out.

The poor animal had been racked with tremors so strong he'd barely been able to remain upright as the veterinarian had checked him over for injuries. One knee was swelling, and he had a gash on his right hip. The doctor didn't think either was a debilitating injury, but he wouldn't know for sure until they'd gotten him back to the clinic and taken some X-rays.

The terrified sounds Laredo had made as he'd struggled to free himself would remain with her for the rest of her life. Along with the sight of that car coming through the intersection and slamming into the Millners' car—the way the trailer had wrenched sideways and flipped to the left, almost taking the car over with it. Everything had happened in slow motion as she'd skidded to a halt with a scream.

Covering her face with her hands, she took deep breaths as she struggled to contain the emotions that were tumbling over and over inside her, trying to get out. If she let go now, she doubted she'd be able to stop. She sucked air in through her nose until her lungs were full, and then forced it back out of her mouth in a slow, controlled hiss, just like a jogger headed into his tenth mile.

Find the rhythm, Trisha. Don't think about anything else. In...two, three, four. Out...two, three, four.

On her tenth breath cycle, the sound of an approaching vehicle made her lower her hands and glance up. Not the tow truck she'd been hoping for, but an expensive-looking car. Great. Instead of going past her, though, it slowed then pulled off the road.

She straightened her spine as the face inside the vehicle came into sharp focus.

Mike. What was he doing here?

Her hand went to her chest. Sarah? Had something terrible happened? Scrambling off the trailer, she practically ran to the car. Mike got out and reached for her just as she stumbled into him, pulling her close. "You okay?"

"I'm fine." She leaned back to look at his face. "Sarah? Is she—?"

"She's okay." He eased her cheek back to his shoulder, his left arm looping around her waist. "Her mom's worried about her horse. What in God's name made you promise to try to take care of it?"

Something about the way he said it made her pause.

Of course...his wife had been killed in some kind of accident involving a horse. But *she* wasn't his wife. She wasn't anything to him.

Maybe it was just the impersonal concern that one

human being might have for another. "I'm fine, Mike. I had to help. Laredo was…he was terrified. Trapped. How could I just leave him there all alone? I couldn't walk away, any more than you could have walked away from one of your patients."

He didn't say anything, but something brushed lightly across the top of her head. His chin? His lips?

After a minute he asked, "How is he?"

"Banged up and bruised, but the vet thinks he'll recover."

"So he's not out at your place?"

"No."

The warm solidness of his chest beneath her cheek calmed her like nothing else could, the slight lingering scent of his aftershave flooding her senses with each breath. He'd come here to find her. Why? To check on Laredo? Because Sarah's mom was worried about him?

Somehow she didn't think that was it. Why, then?

Maybe it was better not to know. Maybe she should just enjoy his presence as she waited for the tow truck to arrive.

"You feel a little shaky. Do you want me to take you home?"

She started to shake her head then realized he couldn't see it the way they were standing. "A tow truck is coming for the trailer. And I have my own vehicle."

The last thing she wanted to do was drive, though. Witnessing that accident…seeing an animal in that condition who'd trusted them to keep him safe was one of the worst things she'd ever gone through—almost worse even than finding out who her husband really was. Worse than having to live the rest of her life in hiding. At least she'd had some power over her own destiny, could understand what was going on. Unlike Laredo. Would he ever allow himself to be loaded into a trailer again after this?

The officer evidently wondered what was going on, because he was suddenly there, asking Mike who he was. Mike explained he was a friend, and that he'd come out to check to see if Trisha was okay.

A friend. Huh. She couldn't remember a friend ever kissing her the way he'd kissed her.

He hadn't mentioned Sarah or her mother when he'd addressed the cop. Or even identified himself as a doctor. Had he really just come out to check on her? As if to verify that, his arm tightened around her and she let her eyes shut as she settled closer, glad not to have to deal with any of this for a few precious seconds. The officer didn't ask anything else, so he must have gone back to his car. They stood that way for a little while, and she'd have been content to stay there for the rest of her life. But she couldn't. Even as she thought it, she heard the wheezing sound of an engine in the distance. This time it was the tow truck, she knew that without even having to look.

She took a deep breath and went to take a step back, only to have Mike grip her a little tighter. "Why don't you sit in my car and I'll take care of this?"

"I'm okay. I need to drive to the hospital as soon as the truck leaves. I want to make sure Sarah is okay."

"She is. I promise. The doctor treating her is a friend. I told him to call me if there was any change."

He didn't insist she get into the car, but stood there with her as she spoke to the driver and got the name of the auto body shop they were taking the truck to. The policeman left as soon as the truck did, the officer giving them a half-wave as he pulled back onto the road.

She wasn't sure what she was supposed to do at this

point. "Thanks for coming out. I'll let you get back to whatever you were doing."

"I'll follow you to the house."

Tugging free, she looked up at him. "I'm sure you have other responsibilities."

"I was just coming off my shift when I got your call, so I'm free for the rest of the day." He gave a small smile. "I have to admit, when you said there'd been an accident I thought Brutus might have gone berserk again."

That's why he'd sounded strained on the phone. "I don't let my students or patients ride him. I told you that."

"Accidents don't always happen while riding."

The tight words weren't referring to Brutus, or to anything involving her.

"No, they don't." She kept her voice soft, hoping he would volunteer more information, but when he dug his hand into his pants pocket and came out with his car keys, she realized he wasn't going to volunteer anything further. "I'll take you up on that offer to follow me home. I'll even make us some coffee, if you'd like some. Besides, I really do want to hear how Sarah is doing, if you don't mind calling the hospital."

"I don't."

He waited for her to climb into her car and start it up before he moved back to his own vehicle. The ride to her little ranch seemed to take forever, but it probably only lasted fifteen minutes. She pulled in beside the barn, suddenly needing to check on her own little herd and make sure they were okay.

"I'll just be a minute," she called, when Mike powered down his window, his brows raised in question.

She slid the door to the barn open, and went in, checking each stall and rubbing Crow's nose when he leaned his head over the door of his stall in greeting. She breathed in the familiar scents that surrounded her, letting them calm her nerves. It was okay. Sarah was going to be fine. Laredo was in good hands. Her own horses were safe. Reaching up, she circled Crow's neck, horrified to find her eyes had filled to overflowing. "It's going to be okay." The words weren't meant for him, they were meant to reassure herself.

Crow's head went up just as a pair of hands landed on her shoulders. She stiffened for a split second then realized it had to be Mike. Allowing her head to lean back against his chest, she scrubbed her palms beneath her eyes. His arms went around her waist, his chin coming to rest on her right shoulder. She felt surrounded and cared for in a way she hadn't for many, many months. This man had no deep dark secrets. Well, he did have one, but she was pretty sure the rest of the town knew about it. She didn't blame him for not wanting to announce it to every newcomer who wandered into Dusty Hills. Her heart ached for him.

"Are you okay?"

She twisted in his arms until she faced him, splaying her hands on his chest. "I will be. I just had to make sure my guys were safe."

A low chuckle rumbled in his chest. "Your guys, huh?"

She smiled back, her world slowly going back into its right orbit. "What? You didn't know I was surrounded by a horde of hungry admirers—emphasis on the hungry part?"

"Oh, I have no doubts you have plenty of male admirers fighting for your attention."

"Not so many." Most of the men she knew weren't her biggest fans. Not any more. But, then, Mike didn't need to know that. "I lead a pretty boring life, in fact."

"I would have to disagree with you there." One of his hands came up, his fingers sliding into the hair at her nape. "Most of my encounters with you have been anything but boring."

True. And most of those encounters had ended up with her falling into his arms. Literally, at times. And once it had ended up with him kissing her.

The memory of that frantic session in the barn washed over her. She wanted that again...wanted his lips on hers, wanted to forget about the horrors of this afternoon, even if just for a few minutes.

As if he'd read her mind, he tilted her head back until their eyes met. He stared at her for several long seconds as if seeking confirmation of something. Then slowly, far too slowly, his head lowered until his lips touched hers. A shard of longing went through her. This was how it was supposed to be between a man and woman: attraction that built until there was no denying it on either side. At least, not on hers. She was attracted. Had been from almost the moment she'd set eyes on him.

His mouth increased its pressure, the hand in her hair holding her in place, not that she had any intention of moving. To emphasize that point, her hands slid up his chest, and she went up on tiptoe to meet him halfway.

Crow had evidently gotten tired of them, because the sound of munching hay came from somewhere behind her. Or maybe that was her horse's way of grabbing a bowl of popcorn and settling in to watch the show.

And she hoped there would be something to see this time.

If she had anything to do with it, the man was not going to run out on her again. No, he was going to stay right here and make her forget that anything else existed but him, and his mouth on hers. But more than that, she wanted him to finish what he'd started yesterday.

CHAPTER SEVEN

NOW WASN'T THE time for this.

Even as the thought went through his head, his hand tightened in Trisha's hair as if his body was declaring mutiny on all things rational.

She's just had a bad scare, you idiot. You need to back off.

Trisha's fingers, which had been resting on his shoulders, suddenly curled around the back of his neck, gripping tight as if she, too, sensed his thoughts.

Not the actions of a woman who wanted him to take a step or two back.

To test that theory, he changed the angle of his mouth, his body soaking up each new sensation. Her lips were soft, sweet...clinging in all the right ways. Ways that made moving back difficult, if not impossible. Ways that made his body harden and his hands itch to explore. For now, though, he focused his attention on that central point of contact, knowing that it could end at any moment.

Maybe he'd be saved by the bell. But the phone at his hip remained silent, no warning chirp or vibration coming to the rescue.

Trisha's body pressed closer, breasts flattening against

his chest, belly coaxing dangerous reactions from a certain part of his anatomy.

To hell with this.

His arm swept around the small of her back, hauling her fully against him, and the intent of the kiss changed—going from hesitant and exploratory to hard and demanding in an instant. His tongue pierced the space between her lips, delving straight and deep, letting her wet heat bathe him, the quick scrape of her teeth only adding to the sharp pleasure.

A small sound came from her throat. Not a panicked squeak at his sudden invasion, but a low hum that urged him to continue. Asked for more.

A request he was only too happy to grant. Using his body, he backed her against the nearest plank wall and crowded her tight against it, never taking his mouth from hers.

Better. Much better. He no longer had to use his hands to bind her to him, and could send them to other places.

Like her breasts.

His fingertips trailed up her waist until he reached the outer swell, gauging her reaction as he reached the uppermost part. He didn't know about hers, but his body's response was instantaneous at even the hint that he might get to hold the weight of those generous curves. His hips angled in closer, the ache inside growing stronger. He forced his hands to continue higher, strumming along the sides of her neck, her whimper and her slight lift onto tiptoe signaling that she wanted his hands back where they had been.

He mentally sought out his wallet…found it in his back pocket, cursing himself for slipping a little something in there after their last encounter. He'd mentally flogged himself for doing so, but had worried about what might happen if things ever got more out of hand. That lack of protection had saved him the last time, but he'd worried about the next. Except that meant that he was even less likely to call a halt to things now.

As if testifying to that fact, he took one step back. Not to stop what he was doing but to do more. His mouth came off hers as his hands retraced their steps with aching slowness. He reached her breasts, but instead of continuing down the sides and heading back to his starting point he took a detour, fingers sliding toward the middle, encountering nipples that were already tight with need.

Trisha's eyelids fluttered shut and her head fell back against the barn wall behind her. She moaned when he allowed his thumbs to linger, passing back and forth over the center of her breasts. She had a bra on, he'd bumped over the edges of it a few seconds earlier, but it was evidently thin, because he could feel everything: the soft fullness; the warmth; that tempting pebbled nipple. In fact, he could go just like this… He curved his right hand, and she filled it to overflowing, arching her back and pressing herself into his touch.

Yes. He squeezed, his other thumb never stopping its sweeping motions.

Her teeth dug into her lower lip, then her eyes opened and she gave a fair imitation of a glare as she settled back against the wall beside Crow's stall. "If you run away again, I'll chase you down and make you finish this."

Run away?

Oh, when he'd left last time.

He gave her a slow smile that he hoped got across his meaning. "I wasn't prepared last time. This time I've got everything I need."

"I'll say." Her brows went up, and her hips rotated forward until she found him.

She wasn't some shrinking violet, he'd say that for her. And that made him even hotter.

He bent, pressing his lips to her neck and biting his way down to her shoulder. She squirmed against him and her fingers curled into his hair, gripping as he continued his quest. Then he was there, wet mouth meeting dry T-shirt-covered nipple and sucking it.

"Ah!" Her handhold on his hair tightened as she arched into his mouth, and he imagined the sensation arrowing straight to her center. Which, if it felt anything like his needy flesh did right now, was kicking up a racket about being ignored. And he did have one free hand...

The waistband of her jeans was snug, but not so tight that he couldn't ease beneath it...like so. Or so tight that he couldn't make his way over the front of her panties—lace, if the texture was anything to go by.

What color?

He bit down on her nipple, hearing her pant near his ear as he held it prisoner, laving his tongue over it. His fingers reached the heat at the juncture of her thighs and everything in his mind scrambled, like a brain suddenly bombarded with too many electrical impulses. The woman's panties were already moist. Wet, in fact. If they were both naked, he could just thrust into that slick channel... and be squeezed into oblivion.

But he might not even make it that far, if he didn't shut down that line of thought.

He allowed himself the luxury of sliding his fingers over her panties, absorbing the gentle bumps and dips that went along with being a woman.

A sharp pain went through his scalp as Trisha suddenly yanked his hair, pulling his head up. "If you don't get this show on the road, I promise you it's going to come crashing to a halt."

Crashing to a halt?

One hand down her pants and the other still on her breast, he blinked at the hint of warning in her tone. He took in her flushed cheeks. Dilated pupils. Uneven breaths.

Maybe she didn't mean crashing to a halt as in she was going to stop him. Maybe she meant crashing as in…exploding.

To test his hypothesis, he rippled his fingertips lightly over the surface of her panties. Her hips jerked forward in response, and she gasped. "Mike, please. You're going to be sorry in a few seconds if you don't stop. I need to get your clothes off."

Her hands left his hair and gripped handfuls of his shirt, tugging, trying to haul it out of his slacks.

Entranced by her frantic movements, he decided to be the devil that realized her worst fear. And he could guarantee he wouldn't be sorry. Not in a million years. Not if the world crashed down on top of him in the next couple of minutes.

Taking his hand from her breast, he caught one of her wrists and then the other, jerking them both away from his shirt and carrying them up over her head. He held them there, his lips curving up in a smile.

"Wh-what are you doing?"

He leaned forward and whispered against her ear. "What do you think I'm doing?" His middle finger trailed along the elastic edge of her panties then ducked beneath it. Her skin was softer than he could have believed. He moved along her folds, getting closer.

"No!" She struggled. "I want you inside me."

His erection jumped at the offer. One he had to refuse. For now.

"Oh, honey, don't worry, I will be. Right about…" his finger pushed inside her in a smooth gliding motion "…now."

She clamped down on him the second he entered her, just like he'd known she would.

"That's not what I meant." Her throaty moan hit his ears, just as her legs parted and she pushed herself further onto him, her body at war with her words.

"Didn't anyone ever tell you you should always say what you mean?" He added another finger, his thumb circling up to find her clit. "Or you could get into deep trouble."

Just like he was. He struggled to hang back from the edge of a steep cliff, even as he worked to push her over it. He wanted to enjoy her climax. Wanted to watch her break apart, holding his own need in check.

Maybe Trisha realized she wasn't going to get her way, or maybe she was just too far gone to care, but her hips rocked forward and back in time with the rhythm of his fingers. It was heady to see her there, fully clothed, arms pinned over her head…a prisoner of his hands and her own passions.

God, she was gorgeous.

He leaned in and bit her lip, before backing away to watch her again. Her eyes were shut tight. Mouth slightly open. Head tipped back against the wall. He doubted she'd even felt that love bite he'd just given her. Well, he bet she'd feel this.

He quickened the pace of his thumb.

Five seconds later he had his answer when her body stiffened, hips moving, moving, moving into his touch. A sharp cried rang out, a horse whinnying in response from one of the stalls, then the walls surrounding his fingers squeezed impossibly tight before releasing again, setting off a series of contractions that had him praying for mercy as he thought about what was in store for him.

His mouth watered, taking in every gasped breath, every muttered word as he continued to move his fingers, slowing the pace as he eased her back down to earth. She finally slumped forward and he released her wrists, his arm coming around her back to support her.

"Oh, God." The whispered words passed over his neck, the warm air no match for the inferno currently raging within his body. She kissed the skin just below his ear. "I told you you'd be sorry."

Was she serious?

"Oh, I'm not sorry. Don't think I am, not even for a second." He smiled, and held her in his arms. "But you may be, as soon as you point me toward the nearest horizontal surface that's not covered in muck."

She laughed, a low throaty sound that went straight to his groin. "What's the matter, cowboy? Do you have something against vertical surfaces? Or are you just vertically challenged?"

With that, she wrapped her fingers around his arms and turned him, until it was him with his back against the warm plank wall she'd just occupied. And then she slowly sank to her knees in front of him.

She was about to exact her revenge. She'd cursed and railed at him inside her head when he'd gotten hold of her hands, and she'd realized what he was about to do. Seconds later, she hadn't much cared, as long as he made those delicious sensations continue. Now she was replete and satisfied and wanted to give back to him. But she wanted to make him suffer. Just a little.

"Trisha—"

"Shh." Her fingers went to the button on his slacks, and she peered up at him as she popped it open. "I may not be strong enough to hold your hands together, like you did mine, but I have a whole lot of leather in this barn. I bet I can find something that would work." The image of a pair of thin supple reins wrapped round and round Mike's wrists, suspending his arms high over his head as she had her way with him flashed through her mind.

To block it out, she eased his zipper down. She'd wanted him inside her, well, now was her chance. It wasn't quite the way she'd envisioned the scene, but sometimes you had to work with what you had, and what she had was...

Her eyes widened at what she found in front of her, and her glance flew up to meet Mike's, noting the quick beat of a muscle in his cheek, the molten look of pure lust. She tugged and pulled on his slacks until they slid down around his ankles. Then slowly she reached up and peeled down his underwear.

Oh, man.

"Trisha." This time there was some kind of desperate plea in his voice. One she recognized. She'd felt the same desperation a few minutes ago.

Opening her mouth, she let her tongue slide slowly over him, letting the taste of his skin wash over her and fill her senses. She'd barely started before a pair of hands dragged her to her feet.

Hard eyes burned into hers. "That's not how this is going to go down."

Keeping hold of her arm, he kicked off his shoes, stepped out of his clothes and reached down to scoop up his pants. Shaking his wallet loose from his back pocket, he flipped it open.

"Condom."

"Let me go, and you can get it."

He shook his head. "I don't trust you for a second. Reach in and get it out."

That whisper at the back of her head was getting louder. Telling her that maybe she hadn't missed out after all. That maybe he'd been right, because the way she was feeling, she might just be capable of pulling a rabbit out of a hat.

Or at least a condom out of a wallet.

She peeked into the main section and caught sight of a foil packet, right next to a hundred-dollar bill—there was a small wad of bills, in fact. A trickle of something went down her spine before it drifted away again. She grabbed the condom, and Mike let the wallet fall to the ground, some of those bills spilling from it. All hundreds.

Right now she didn't care how much money the man did or didn't have. She only wanted one thing.

This time he did let go of her, and she opened the packet—on her first try!—and started to hand it to him. Only to have him shake his head and curve both hands over her breasts and squeeze gently. A familiar shaft of need bloomed in her belly and spread outward. Down-ward.

"My hands are full," he murmured.

And hers were now shaking, but somehow she managed to get it out of the package and roll it over him.

The second it was on, he used his grip on her breasts to reverse their positions—she was back against the wall. Mike yanked off his shirt and then reached for hers, pulling it off in one smooth move. Her pants and boots followed, leaving her standing there in her bra and underwear.

"Red. Very nice. I expected something plain and simple."

She glanced down, noting he was staring at her bra and underwear. Both lacy and red, neither doing much to conceal her from his view. "You'd prefer granny panties?"

"Honey, right now I'd take you in long johns. But I am going to take you."

The intensity behind his voice set off a firestorm of want. All over again.

"I thought you wanted a horizontal surface," she said, the breathiness in her voice sounding strange and alien.

"And I remember you questioning my abilities with regard to vertical ones." With that, he slid his hands down her hips and grasped the back of each of her thighs, just below her butt, and hauled her up. "So wrap your legs around me and get ready to hold on tight."

She tightened her legs and he walked a step or two, until the planks were at her back again. He pulled aside the elastic of her panties, until she felt him at her entrance. He then bit back a short curse—or maybe it was a prayer?—and burst into her in a single powerful thrust.

The impact of their bodies colliding sent the air whistling from her lungs as he entered her again and again. Her position gave her no control over the depth or speed, and it drove her wild to have him finally take what he wanted from her. And he wanted it deep. Mind-shatteringly deep.

He stopped suddenly, still inside her, one hand beneath her right thigh. He planted the other flat against the wall next to her shoulder. Her calves tightened when he continued to stand there motionless.

"Are—are you done?"

Oh, Lord, she hoped not.

"Are you serious?" He surged forward as if to show her exactly how wrong she was. "But I forgot about the wood. Is it hurting your back?"

"Are *you* serious?" Okay, yes, she was probably going to have some serious abrasions and maybe a splinter or two, but all she knew was that he was mashing just the right spot. She wiggled on his length, contracting her muscles and letting the hot sensation of fullness wash over her.

He let out another groaned curse. "Now that that's settled…" He planted his mouth on hers and thrust his tongue into her mouth, then he followed it with his body, a kind of echo and response that had her closing her eyes and doing as he'd suggested—holding on tight.

Again and again, his pelvic bone hitting that bud of sensitive tissue with each pass. Mouth…pelvis…mouth… pelvis. Between the two of them something was always in motion, leaving her no time to snatch a breath or pause to recover. Instead, the whine of tension inside her grew more shrill with each dueling cadence until it reached the top rung of the scale and held like an opera singer on that final shrieking note of the climax. Her fingernails dug into Mike's shoulders harder than she could have dreamed possible as an explosion from inside her body obliterated all sound. In a vacuum of silence she fell and fell, even as Mike's mouth left hers and she sensed him shouting, the veins standing out in his neck even as she continued her rapid descent.

A few seconds passed before a few vague sounds filtered back through her eardrums. Then a forehead pressed to hers. Their breathing wasn't in sync, but random snatches of air said he was as affected as she was.

Lord. That was…that was…

There were no words.

She flattened her fingers on his shoulders, hoping she hadn't broken the skin.

Mike took a step back, still holding her, and allowed her legs to slide back to the earth as he eased from her.

Swallowing, she tried to recover her scattered thoughts, just as Mike's low voice intruded. "Are you okay?"

Was she?

She had no idea. Although she suspected that if his arm wasn't behind her back, supporting her, she'd probably fall down in a heap.

She hoped she hadn't broken something.

That "something' now included more than the skin on his shoulders.

She sincerely hoped she hadn't just broken her own heart.

CHAPTER EIGHT

MIKE DISLIKED TWO things in life: lies…and horses.

He leaned back in his chair and tossed his pencil onto the desk.

He could swear that brute horse of hers had glared at him yesterday as he'd exited the barn post haste. But the glassy-eyed look Trisha had given him as he'd asked her if she was okay had spooked him. Or had it been the sex?

Yeah, that's what it was. The two women he'd been with in the weeks after his wife's death had seemed happy with quick animalistic mating sessions. Sessions that had left him unmoved. A tiny part of him wondered if the sex had been his way of getting revenge on his wife for what she'd done behind his back. Cheating on her memory, the way she'd cheated on him. That fact had upped the guilt he'd felt afterwards, because she was no longer there to debate the issue, or tell her side of the story.

His time with Trisha hadn't been about revenge. Not at all. In fact, it had been…

Something else. Something he didn't want to examine. And most certainly something he didn't want to repeat.

She'd pulled back from him quickly, grabbing her clothes and yanking them on. Her shirt had been inside out when she'd finished, but he hadn't been about to tell her that, and Trisha hadn't seemed to notice. She'd given him a quick smile and asked if he'd be there for Clara's session on Thursday. When he'd stepped forward with an outstretched hand to touch her, she'd taken a quick step back and waved him away. "I've got to get back to work."

As if what they'd done hadn't left her legs shaking like it had his.

Vertical spaces should be outlawed.

Because never had he lifted a woman onto his hips and slammed her against a wall, thinking about nothing but getting as close as he could—until about halfway through, when a flash of something rational had made him wonder if he was peeling the skin off her back with each thrust.

She had assured him he wasn't.

He dragged a hand through his hair before tipping his head back and staring at the ceiling. In all his thirty-four years he couldn't remember feeling this bone-rattling need for a woman.

Not even Marcy.

That first kiss in the arena had built this whole thing up in his mind until it had become a train wreck, just waiting for the opportunity to career into the nearest... wall.

He laughed. He had to stop thinking about that barn wall. And slamming into it again and again.

He blew out a rough breath and turned his attention back to his desk, seeing the framed photo he kept there as a reminder. Marcy and her horse. Another train wreck waiting to happen. Why couldn't the local hippotherapist's name be Raul, or Beefy Bones Bart.

Why the hell had it been Trisha who'd landed on his doorstep, with her smile and her saucy comments?

Maybe this time would be different.

Different how? He'd known Marcy his whole life, yet in the end he'd found he hadn't known her at all.

He didn't even know where Trisha was from. In fact, she'd been evasive about everything from her references—which she never had given him, like she'd promised—to where she'd lived in the past. He couldn't help but feel she was hiding something. She hadn't volunteered one scrap of information that he hadn't asked for, and even then her answers had been purposely vague. Or was he just being paranoid because of Marcy?

Just as he was about to get up to go on another set of rounds, his phone rang.

If that was her…

Nope, his readout said R. Chapman. Ray. Nothing to do with Trisha. He frowned. Unless there'd been another accident.

His heart started pounding, despite the ridiculousness of the idea. "Hi, Ray, what's up?"

"Just checking in, like I said I would. Your hippotherapist doesn't have any open warrants. Or any convictions that I could find."

Mike was lost for a second, before he remembered he'd asked the sheriff to check on Trisha. The whole thing seemed preposterous and paranoid now. Kind of like this constant gnawing worry. Then his friend's tone came through. It was off somehow.

"What is it?"

"Nothing. I didn't find anything of concern."

A wave of foreboding rolled through him. "Come on, Ray. These are my patients we're talking about. If you know something and one of them gets hurt because you held out on me, you and I are going to have a serious problem."

There was a pause, and Mike could imagine his friend

struggling with all the ethical ramifications of his job. "I'm only telling you this because you could find the same information online, if you looked. Her certifications don't hold up. At least, not under the name Patricia Bolton."

"What?" The realization hit his stomach with a sickening thud. "Maybe she's listed under Trisha."

"There are a few Boltons, but the addresses don't match. Do you know where she lived before Dusty Hills?"

No. Because she'd refused to give him any references that weren't from her current location. He'd sensed something was wrong from the moment he'd asked. The memory of her fear during their first meeting came back... the way she'd held that curved tool. "No idea. Can you give me some numbers to call?"

"I can, but you won't find anything. It's as if she's a ghost. You can follow her trail for a while. It'll even lead you on a merry little chase, over a few hills, around a few curves, but after a while it just peters out cold. Her plates come up, but they list an address in Reno—only that address doesn't exist. Same thing with her driver's license."

"What the hell?" He only realized the words came out as a shout when his door opened and his receptionist peeked inside the office. He waved her away with what he hoped was a reassuring smile but which felt more like a snarling twist of lips. As soon as the door closed again, he focused on what Ray was saying. "What does it mean?"

"I have no idea. Could be she's a felon on the run who changed her name. Or a battered wife hiding from her husband. Maybe those guys who came to town with her that day were helping her get away from something."

Crap. He had just had sex with a possible felon? Perfect. Only Trisha didn't feel like a criminal.

As if you would know. Then again, four years ago he would have sworn his wife was faithful and true.

He didn't know anything right now. Like whether he should let his old friend know he'd been consorting with her.

Consorting. He let out an audible snort.

"What?" Ray had evidently heard him. "Something I should know?"

What if Trisha really was married? The horse trainer who'd had an affair with his wife hadn't known she'd had a husband—he'd been as shocked as Mike had been to find out the truth. A creeping sense of nausea wove through his gut.

Was Trisha pulling one over on him? She had a class ring on that finger, but what if she wore it to hide the mark left by a gold band? "You didn't happen to find out if she was married, did you?"

"Nope." There was a pause. "Mike. Tell me you didn't. I told you not to get involved with her."

He wanted to tell his friend he hadn't. But he'd gone out there with a condom in his wallet. If that wasn't premeditation, he didn't know what was. As much as he might try to rationalize this thing, the evidence was there. He'd known there was a possibility he might sleep with her.

But what if she'd lied to him? About more than just her marital status?

It made the flip playfulness that he'd thought was so hot take on a more sinister tone. Like a taunt from the serpent in the garden.

Are you vertically challenged?

"Mike. You there?"

"Yeah." He shifted away from his friend's original question. "Just a little shocked. She wanted to treat some of my patients, so now I don't know what to think. Thanks for letting me know. I think I need to have a long talk with the lady in question."

"Don't do anything stupid."

Too late for that. But he could start playing this thing a whole lot smarter from here on out.

"I'll keep that in mind, Ray."

As soon as he got off the phone, his gaze fell on his wife's picture. Reaching for it, stared at it…ran his fingers over the cold glass covering Marcy's face. He'd loved her, no matter what she'd done.

Maybe it had been up to him to talk to her, to make sure she was happy. But he'd been so busy with his work back then, he'd barely had time to stop and breathe, let alone sit down and really listen to his wife.

Would you have told me, if I'd asked?

Whether the telepathic question reached her or not, he had no way of knowing. All he knew was that there was a fierce burning in his chest that had nothing to do with lust right now. He knew what he had to do tomorrow at Clara Trimble's hippotherapy session.

He was going to ask, and hope he received answers to a few very important questions.

And if he didn't like what he heard?

His jaw tightened until it was a mass of tense ligaments and hard muscle. If she lied to him again, he was going to withdraw his recommendation for Clara's treatment. And then he was going to make sure everyone in town knew that Patricia Bolton was a liar and a fraud.

"How are you feeling, honey?" Trisha tucked back a strand of Sarah's hair, glancing again at the door to her student's hospital room and praying Mike didn't come sweeping in. She still didn't know how she was going to face him after what they'd done yesterday. Trisha had once considered herself a happy person who liked to laugh and have fun. That had all changed when she'd discovered who her husband was. His accusations about her sleeping with the hired help...her shock when Roger had shot the man in cold blood.

In fact, she hadn't felt happy in a long, long time. Until yesterday.

She'd just started letting her hair down in Dusty Hills after six long months of being vigilant—of fearing for the safety of her family. But nothing had happened in the days following her husband's conviction. Maybe it was time for her to stop being so afraid and finally start living her life again.

But did she really have to start out by having wild sex in the barn? Her teeth came together, grinding a time or two as she remembered those heated moments. Had she really called him vertically challenged?

Yeah. She had. And it was pretty much the best thing she'd ever done in her life. Her jaws relaxed, and her mouth curved.

"I'm doing okay," Sarah said, bringing her back to the present. "Still hurts quite a bit." She struggled to shift higher in her bed, and Trisha hurried to help her get comfortable. "Have you heard anything about how Laredo's doing?"

She'd meant to check on him yesterday, but had wound up in Mike's arms instead. She'd ended up calling the vet that morning. "He's a little banged up, just like you. But you'll both be fine before you know it."

At least, she hoped so. Once Laredo was strong enough to be loaded into a trailer without being tranquilized, like he had at the scene of the accident, would he do so willingly?

Maybe he'd bounce right back, like she seemed to be doing lately. She hadn't thought of her ex and what he might or might not do for the last week or so. How convenient that it was right about the time she'd started getting to know a certain sexy neurosurgeon. From whom she hadn't heard a peep. Not since their encounter. She glanced again at the door.

Maybe he was feeling as awkward as she was and wasn't sure what to say to her.

She couldn't imagine Mike having random bouts of shyness. Not after what he'd done to her—after what he'd said.

Then again, she'd said some pretty wild things herself. She'd die if he ever repeated them to anyone.

He won't. He's not the kind to kiss and tell.

As if she were an expert on what the man would or wouldn't say—or any man, for that matter. Everything about Roger-slash-Viktor had been a lie.

Just like your life here in Dusty Hills.

Except she wasn't a killer.

But she was a liar. *Only out of necessity.*

The door behind her opened, and Trisha turned, expecting to see Sarah's mom, who'd stepped out to call a few relatives and give them an update. Instead, it was the last person she wanted to see right now.

Heat flooded her face and she opened her mouth to greet him, only to find that nothing came out. She snapped her jaws shut and settled for nodding to him instead.

He didn't say anything to her at first, just chatted with Sarah about how she was doing. Still not looking Trisha's way, he flipped through his patient's chart, asking questions as he perused whatever was written there.

He finally turned toward her. "Ms. Bolton, I didn't expect to see you here today."

Uh-oh. Last name. Not a good sign. Maybe because it was a public place, and he wanted to maintain an appearance of professionalism. That was a possibility… except for the heavy layer of frost she now sensed in the room. "Sarah's my student, and I care about her. Where else would I be?"

A beat or two passed as he studied her, eyes narrowed. "I wouldn't know, actually."

What was that supposed to mean?

She shook herself. Time to stop second-guessing every word that came out of his mouth. He was probably doing exactly the same thing with her. Maybe she should try to ease the awkwardness. Or lay the reason for it on the table and see what he did. "So what did you do yesterday? Anything interesting?"

Holding her breath, she watched his reaction. Right on cue, a dark wave of red washed up his neck and into his face. But not even that made him break into a smile. "I did all kinds of things. Made a few phone calls…learned some things I didn't know."

Things about her? The frost in the room seeped into her soul. "What kinds of things?"

He shrugged. "Things that are best left for a later discussion. Know this: my patients' well-being is very important to me." Pointedly glancing in Sarah's direction, Trisha noted that, despite her pain medication, she was looking at them with open curiosity.

He was right. This wasn't the time to discuss what had happened. But why was he warning her about his patients? Did he think she would do something to compromise that?

Or worse, did he think she'd had sex with him expecting to receive those referrals in return? The thoughts she'd had after that first kiss came back to haunt her.

Surely not! But the sooner she cleared that up, the better. She stood and crossed over to Sarah, kissing her on the cheek. "I need to go back to the barn and take care of the horses, and I have another student this afternoon. But I'll be back in the morning, okay?"

Sarah nodded and gave a huge yawn. Poor thing. The teenager had to be exhausted, and here she was having to listen to her and Mike lobbing obscure comments back and forth.

She walked out of the room, not looking behind her. Mike had evidently followed her, because her name rang out above the noise of the busy hospital floor. "Hold up for a second."

Halting in her spot, she waited for him to continue. He did better than that, however, he circled in front of her. "We do need to talk about a few things, and I have some questions."

"I can stop off for some coffee at the cafeteria, if you want to join me."

A cool smile met her invitation. "I don't think you want anyone overhearing this particular conversation."

Oh, God, it *was* about their encounter yesterday. That was the only discussion she could think of that he'd want to keep quiet. He either regretted what they'd done—*really* regretted it—or she was right on her more paranoid imaginings that he thought she was after something and was using sex to get it.

She *had* been after something. His body. Nothing more.

A faint whisper wove through the back of her skull. She ignored it, drawing herself upright. "Okay. So where do you want to discuss this—whatever *this* is?"

"How about after Clara Trimble's session? I'd like to observe her."

"Fine. I don't have any more patients scheduled afterward."

A glimmer of something that might have been anger went through his eyes. "Speaking of patients, how is your client list looking these days?"

She gulped down a ball of dismay.

Stall, Trisha, until you know what this is about. "It's about where I'd expect it to be for someone who's only been here for six months."

A couple of blips sounded from his phone. He glanced at the readout, then back up at her. "There's an emergency. I need to go. I'll see you at Clara's session."

She murmured a goodbye and watched him stride down the hallway. Then she turned and headed toward the nearest exit, stepping into the hot Nevada sunshine.

But even the bright day couldn't chase away the storm clouds that rolled around inside her, clouds that were growing blacker by the minute. She had a feeling that things between her and Mike were about to take a drastic turn.

Scratch that. From the look on his face as they'd stood outside of Sarah's room, they already had.

The only question was why.

"What have we got?"

The gurney stopped just long enough for Mike to peer beneath one eyelid of the unconscious accident victim and then the other, before they continued to move quickly toward the surgical suite. Pupils were equal and reactive, but there was an obvious knot on the left side of the victim's skull.

"Ten-year-old male with a fractured pelvis and right

wrist, as well as possible ruptured spleen. That's a pretty nasty lump on his head, so we're probably looking at a concussion as well," Peyton recited. "Fell while trying to retrieve a kite from a tree. Met a few branches on the way down. His mother's on her way."

Crap. Kids always thought they were impervious to harm, venturing further and further into the danger zone until it was too late.

Yeah, well, he might as well point that finger right back at himself. He'd ventured into dangerous territory several times recently. It looked like it had finally caught up with him. Trisha had gazed at him with those big green eyes as if she didn't have a clue what he was talking about.

Good try, lady. He couldn't wait to see her face when she realized she'd gotten caught in a web of lies.

If they really were lies. Maybe Ray had been wrong. Maybe she was who she said she was but simply hadn't shown up on his friend's databases.

The day of their first meeting came back to him. Maybe it really was an abusive ex. In which case his anger was totally off base.

He couldn't help but think it was more than that, however.

"Want me to scrub up for surgery?" he asked Peyton.

"We need to get the internal bleeding under control first, but stay close to the hospital for the next couple of hours."

"I'm on duty until eleven. Just give me a yell as soon as you're ready for my evaluation."

The other doctor took hold of the side of the bed and quickened his pace. "Will do. I'll keep you in the loop."

Two hours later Mike was back at the patient's bedside in Recovery, going over the results of the CT scan.

Dexter Barkley had a linear skull fracture about three centimeters long as well as a concussion, but there were no active brain bleeds and the swelling was under control with meds. Sporting a cast on his wrist, the kid had been lucky in that his fractured pelvis had been stable enough to be managed without surgery, although it had taken a couple of hours in the ER to repair the damage to his spleen and wrist.

Poor kid. The next several weeks weren't going to be a picnic. The funny thing was, if he hadn't known what to look for, he'd have sworn Dexter had escaped with just a bump on the noggin and a little arm cast. But, as these things often were, there had been a lot more going on just below the surface, in places you couldn't see without specialized equipment.

Like Trisha? She looked perfectly normal on the surface. But what was beneath that playful, sexy facade?

He tried to shake free of that thought. He'd thought of the hippotherapist far too often this afternoon. He could only hope Clara's session brought some answers. Ones that could put his mind at ease.

And if it turned out to be a false alarm, what then? Was he going to go on as if nothing had ever happened between them?

A little voice inside of him said that's exactly what he should do. Rewind the clock and start over—make sure she knew that he wasn't interested in a relationship or anything else...horizontal or vertical.

He rolled his eyes, because as soon as he'd gotten home from the barn yesterday he'd retrieved a box from his medicine cabinet and plucked out a foil-wrapped packet. Into his wallet it had gone. He was aware of its presence with every step he took—and every time he took money out to pay for something. There it was, winking up at him like an omen of things to come.

Oh, yeah. The genie was not only out of the bottle, he was currently vacationing on a sunny little beach in the Bahamas with no return date in sight.

That left Mike with a big problem. He wanted Trisha again. Seeing her that morning had driven a fist to his gut and left him winded. He still couldn't quite catch his breath. He could always say "one more time" and hope that would be the end of it, but he knew better. As soon as he'd had her, he'd want her again. And again.

Despite what she might or might not be hiding.

CHAPTER NINE

TRISHA'S PALMS MOISTENED for the hundredth time as she slowly led Crow around the outside edge of the round pen.

Pressing her left hand against the soft fabric of her worn jeans to blot it, she prayed Mike didn't notice how nervous she was. So far the therapy session had gone without a hitch. Clara hadn't cried or been frightened as they'd placed her on the horse's back. And right now, with Penny walking alongside the child and murmuring encouraging words, it looked like any other successful treatment program.

Except for the man standing on the other side of the fence, watching them with brooding eyes. He'd briefly spoken to Clara's mom, but they now stood on opposite sides of the pen, not because Doris had moved away but because Mike had.

As they neared his location, Trisha's heart rate sped up, as it had every other time they'd passed him. This was ridiculous. It wasn't as if this man could make or break her business. Even if he refused to refer any more patients to her, she'd just go to someone else. Someone in one of the other nearby towns. Surely there were doctors who'd worked with equine therapists before.

Mike wasn't the only neurologist on the block.

She drew to a halt alongside him and forced her voice into what she hoped was a calm but confident tone. "Any questions so far?" She glanced at Penny, who was currently showing Clara how to thank the large animal.

"None that I can think of. At least, none that involve Clara." He gave a small wave to the child, who was now grinning widely at him. "Nice to see you really do make everyone say thank you. I thought I was a special case."

He *was* a special case. And he made her chest ache in a way she didn't understand. But she needed to keep this as casual as possible. The man still hadn't thawed completely. But he'd at least lightened up a little bit. That had to be something, right?

"Like I told you, everyone deserves a thank-you every once in a while." She smiled at her assistant. "Do you want to trade places?"

Penny shook her head. "I'm fine. Besides, Clara's my new buddy." The child reached up with her good arm and patted her black riding helmet, her tiny hand making a slapping sound. Penny guided her fingers back to the straps attached to the front of the saddle. "Don't forget to hold on. Crow's going to start walking in a minute."

A soft cluck to let the horse know they were ready, and the team moved away, stopping on the other side of the ring to speak with Clara's mother, who seemed delighted with how active a role her child was taking. "I've haven't seen her this interested in anything in months. Remind me to thank Dr. Dunning for giving us the okay."

A half-hour later Trisha and Penny lifted Clara from the special saddle and set her on the ground next to the horse, supporting her between the two of them. Crow's head swept down and around, blowing softly through his nostrils when Clara held out her hand. Mike watched from a distance, his hands gripping the rail of the fence. Soon Penny led Crow away to get his well-deserved rub-down and a flake of hay and the barn emptied out as Doris loaded her daughter into the van and pulled out of the driveway. Larry came out of one of the stalls and, after glancing their way, made himself scarce, maybe sensing something was up.

And it was. Mike had evidently not forgotten what-ever it was he wanted to discuss with her, because he said, "Let's walk."

"Okay. We can go to the house. I have some lemonade made, if you want some." She was not above plying him with drink, even if it was the sans alcohol kind.

"Thanks. That sounds good."

As they headed out of the barn, she tried once again to assess his mood, but the man was locked tight. He wasn't quite as icy as he'd been at the hospital, but there was still a tension in his neck and shoulders that made her nervous. Her uneasiness increased when she invited him inside the house and he opted to remain on the porch instead, hands shoved deep in his pockets, while she went to fetch the lemonade.

Afraid of being alone with her?

Well, Penny and Larry would be leaving soon so, in-side the house or outside, they would still be on their own. Maybe it was better to get whatever was on his mind out in the open.

Setting the tray with their drinks on a white wicker table flanked by a couple of matching chairs, she eased into the one across from him. "So," she said, picking up one of the glasses and taking a quick sip, "what did you think of the session?"

"Impressive. But that's not what I want to talk to you about."

"Okay. Let's hear it." If he apologized for their time together, he might just end up wearing his lemonade instead of drinking it.

Mike leaned back in his chair and took a long pull from his glass, swallowing with powerful movements of his throat. He then set the remainder on the table and leaned forward, planting his elbows on his knees. His eyes held hers without blinking. "Who are you?"

The words were soft. Even. With no hint of anger or irritation behind them.

"Excuse me?" Her mind scrambled away from the question, looking for a logical explanation that didn't mean what she thought it did. She'd assumed he wanted to talk to her about what had happened between them in the barn. Instead, it might be about something worse. Much worse.

His gaze never wavered. "You heard me. Who are you?"

She licked her lips, deciding to set her own drink down before she dropped it. A tremor went through her. She'd assumed she was safe. Had Roger somehow contacted him—or someone who worked for him? "I—I don't know what you mean."

"Let's start with your full name."

Oh, God, it *was* what she thought it was. "You already know my name."

"No. I know the name you gave me. And I remember asking for references from your past. You made excuses, if I remember right."

The Feds had warned her about keeping the same job. But it would have been the same no matter what profession she chose. Somewhere along the line someone would want to know where she'd lived, what she'd done, who she'd worked for in her past. What was she going to do? She could call her contacts and ask them to move her again pronto.

And the next time this happened? Was she going to call them every time she got spooked, or each time someone got a little too close to the truth? Was she going to run like a criminal for the rest of her life?

If that's what it took to keep her family safe. Yes.

"I have your references in the house. Let me get them." But this time she couldn't quite meet his eyes when she said it.

"I *trusted* you with my patients' lives."

That stung. And he was right. He'd trusted her to be who she'd said she was.

"I promise you, I am a licensed physical therapist and hippotherapist."

"So you've said. But there's no record of a Patricia Bolton on any of those registries."

He hadn't raised his voice. Not once. And yet every word licked at her flesh like a cat-o'-nine-tails.

"Y-you checked?"

He shifted in his chair. "Can you blame me?"

"No." If she could slip between the wooden planks on her porch she would. No matter what the Feds said, she'd lied to this man. Had put his patients in danger, for all he knew…although he'd let her go ahead with Clara's session, so he must have some doubts about what he was accusing her of.

"When we first talked, something didn't quite seem right, so I asked Sheriff Chapman to do a quick background check. Turns out your name is—"

"You know what it is?" Panic flushed through her system in a torrent, robbing her lungs of air, her brain of thought. When she finally remembered to breathe, it came in with an awful wheezing gasp that she couldn't seem to control. Mike's face zoomed out and then back in.

"Hey." He was crouched beside her in an instant, pushing her head down between her knees. "Take slow breaths…in…out…"

He kept murmuring, but she couldn't focus on anything except what she needed to do. Who had the sheriff told? Who had he asked? Had the information traveled back to the prison in Virginia? Not even her mom or her brother knew where she was.

"Trisha." His hands cupped her cheeks and he made her look at him. "You need to slow your breathing or you're going to pass out."

She realized she was still pulling in air at an alarming rate and her whole body was trembling. The last thing she wanted to do was wind up in a hospital bed where anyone could get to her. Meeting Mike's eyes, she allowed him to direct her when to breathe, even though her chest was burning and the panic inside her threatened to swallow her whole. She blanked everything out except the sound of his voice. The world slowly came back into focus.

Blinking, she found his worried gaze on her. "Welcome back," he said.

She drew a careful breath. "Sorry. I don't know what happened."

"What the hell is going on, Trisha? Did someone threaten you? Hurt you?"

Yes. Her husband. In more ways than one. It dawned on her that Mike hadn't exactly said he knew what her name was. She'd just blurted out the question before he'd even finished his sentence. It would be so easy to say yes, that someone had beat her time and time again until she'd finally run away. But she couldn't bring herself to add one more lie onto the heap.

"No." She squeezed his hands then let go. "I'm okay, thank you."

She waited until he got back into his seat before asking, "What did the sheriff say?"

"That your identity is a little thin." He hesitated. "Are you running from the law?"

That got a laugh out of her. No, she was running *because* of the law. Because someone else had done some very bad stuff, and she'd been forced into hiding. The price to pay for making a huge mistake and trusting someone you shouldn't.

I trusted you with my patients' lives.

No wonder he'd checked up on her. If she'd done the same thing before getting involved with Roger, she'd have probably saved herself and the people around her a whole lot of heartache. And she never would have met Mike, or Sarah, or Clara, or any of the other people she was coming to love— *Yikes!* To care for.

Care. For.

While she did love Sarah and Clara and her other clients, she didn't love Mike. Not even close.

She brought herself back to his question. "No, I'm not running from the law."

"Are you married?"

She swallowed. "No."

Not any more.

As if reading her thoughts, he asked, "*Were* you married?"

Her thumb went to her finger to make sure her fake class ring was still in place, then she stood up in a hurry. "I'm not married. I never would have spent that time with you in the barn if I were."

Something dark passed through his eyes. "That doesn't always stop people."

Her chin went up. "Well, it would stop me."

"Maybe, but that still doesn't answer my original question." He stood as well, hands on the table. "So I'll ask it again. Who are you?"

She closed her eyes, the tight lines of suspicion on his face making her heart ache and her stomach churn.

I want to tell you, Mike. Please, believe me.

It was on the tip of her tongue, in fact, to say it. *I'm in the witness protection program.* But he'd already talked to the sheriff about her. All it would take was a single phone call to start an avalanche that could bury not only her...but him. Literally. Along with her mom. Her brother.

Roger had already killed once because of her. He'd love nothing better than to crush her under his heel, along with anyone close to her. In fact, it might give him more pleasure to hurt someone she cared about and make her live with the knowledge that she was the cause. Even if she told Mike the truth, Sheriff Chapman was sure to come back with either more information or to ask Mike some hard questions. Did she want Mike to have to lie for her?

No. That was her burden and hers alone.

She opened her eyes and took a fortifying breath. "I can't tell you." The words came out as a whisper.

Using her tongue to moisten her lips, she held her hands out from her sides. "Please. Oh, God, Mike, please, believe me. *This* is me. The person standing before you. The person in the barn. All me. The person who worked with Clara...and Sarah." She put every ounce of sincerity she possessed into her words. "I kissed you. Me. *Me!* And I'd do it all over again... I would. I only wish..."

The cracking of her voice on that last word prevented her from going any further.

It evidently spurred Mike into action. He rounded the table and grabbed her, his eyes boring into hers for what seemed like an eternity before his mouth came crashing down, covering hers in a searing kiss that snatched away any last thoughts of saving herself. Of telling him to get off her property and take his precious referrals with him.

Because she didn't want him to go. She wanted him to stay. Wanted *this*.

The hard wooden railing of the wraparound porch was at her back, digging into her flesh, as Mike continued to kiss her as if he couldn't get enough. Well, neither could she. His arm went around her and he was lifting her up until she was sitting on the railing, legs splayed with him between them, pressing hard.

She arched back as he hit just the right spot, her hands scrambling to hang onto the post next to her as he gripped her hips, holding tight as he ground against her again.

Penny and Larry knew to leave when they were done. They wouldn't come round to this side of the house. And, God, she needed him. Needed him so badly she was shaking. On the verge of coming right then and there.

"Please."

As if he knew exactly what she was talking about, he hauled her back off the rail and set her on the ground. He ripped open the button on her jeans and shoved her pants and bikini panties down her hips. Too late, she realized they wouldn't come off without her boots.

Mike didn't try to remove them, however, he just spun her around until the rail was against her belly, and she heard the tell-tale zip of his jeans. The quick ripping of a packet. Then he was bending her over the banister. Thrusting inside. The breath left her lungs, and she saw stars. Mike's hands went to the rail on either side of her rib cage as he entered her again and again in a frenzy that matched everything she felt inside. He didn't try to touch her. There was no foreplay. No sweet nothings. No sounds at all, other than their breathing. But she was burning up inside. She parted her legs as much as she was able, gripping the wooden balusters below, needing him deeper. Harder.

He obliged, withdrawing almost completely and then suddenly lunging forward, hitting something inside her and sending a mixture of pleasure and pain rocketing through her belly.

God, yes!

Again. She wanted that again.

He reared back, then entered her with another powerful stroke of his hips. This time she cried out, but didn't try to stop him. Couldn't. Her toes curled inside her boots as she held on.

A third time. Deep. Hard.

Shattering.

Her eyes slammed closed, she stiffened and... *There! Oh!* Her body went off, a guttural moan forced up from deep inside as she contracted down tight and then spasmed open again and again, sharp pleasure washing over her as he strained inside her, keeping firm pressure on that tender spot. He must have climaxed as well, because he was no longer moving.

A minute or two later, he released the tension, his hands sliding down her arms, kissing the back of her neck.

Lord. She'd never felt so utterly satisfied in all her life.

Mike's fingers linked with hers and he squeezed gently, the act pushing her digits together and sending an ache through her ring finger.

What was he thinking? Was he still hung up on her identity? He'd said nothing as he'd taken her, and it was the way she'd wanted it. But now…

The last thing she wanted to do was lie to him. But she also didn't want to put him in danger by telling him the truth.

"Mike—"

"Shh. It's okay." He pressed his lips to her ear. "Did I hurt you?"

She smiled, relief washing through her when his voice came through warm and mellow. Not a trace of frost remained. "No. Couldn't you tell?"

"I'm glad." He chuckled. "Well that's *two* verticals."

"Mmm." She let her breath out in a sigh. "I'd call that a modified vertical."

"Would you?" His teeth nipped her earlobe. "Your people aren't going to come up on us anytime soon, are they?"

"No. They normally leave straight from the barn."

Mike eased back and slid free, and Trisha immediately missed the closeness. But it wasn't like they could just stay there forever.

"I have to get back to the office."

The regret in his voice made her smile widen. "So who's keeping you?"

"Witch." He slapped her bare butt with enough force to make her yelp. "So now that we've proved I'm not vertically challenged, I say we move on to something else."

"Like?" Her feeling of relief grew, making her feel slightly giddy, although she had a feeling that would fade soon enough. Once reality crept back in. But for now, she held it at bay with a single shake of her fist.

"I was thinking of doing something horizontal." He hauled her to a standing position and turned her around.

Her gaze went straight to the heart of the matter and then back to his face. "Now?"

He leaned in and kissed her before zipping himself back in with a pained groan. Then he reached down and tugged her clothes back up around her hips, sliding up the zipper and fastening her button. "Work, remember? Think 'delayed gratification.'" But know this, Trisha—or whatever your name may be. The next time I have you it's going to be on a nice soft bed." His voice sank to a silky drawl that made her stomach tighten. "I definitely want the bed. It's going to last all night. And those clothes are going to finally come off that delectable body. One piece at a time."

CHAPTER TEN

"I'D LIKE YOU to meet with Clara's treatment team."

Mike's voice came over the phone, the clipped words bearing no resemblance to the velvety promise he'd left her with two days ago. Just as well, since she'd pretty much decided there was no need to adjust the vertical or the horizontal. There would be no repeat performance, even if the thought of what they'd done made her mouth water and her stomach quiver. She'd never craved a man like she craved Mike. Nor had she ever before enjoyed pushing her own sexual boundaries like she did with him.

Having sex in the open…on her porch? That had been stupid. And exciting. And…stupid. The fingers of her free hand went to her nose and pinched hard in an effort to jerk herself back to the present.

As heady as sex with Mike was, how could she even consider getting involved with him when she had to hide things from her past? It was one thing when he'd thought she was who she said she was. It was another thing entirely when he knew her identity was fake. When he knew *she* was fake.

One lapse in judgment could be considered a mistake. Two lapses…temporary insanity. But if she made it to three? That was being *involved*.

"Why do you want me there?"

"I could give you all kinds of reasons."

Her breath caught. But try as she might, she caught no hint of double meaning behind his words. "Name one."

"You're working with Clara. I'd say that makes you part of her team. I want you to explain your philosophy and objectives to the rest of the group. As time goes on, we can appraise whether your line of treatment is yielding results." He paused. "Besides, I've seen you in action. I think you might be on to something."

She straightened next to the stall she'd been mucking. He'd implied she'd no longer be working with his patients if she didn't 'fess up to her real identity. She had to wonder why he'd suddenly decided to include her in his inner circle. Trying to keep an eye on her?

He said he thought she might be on to something though. A warm feeling spread through her stomach.

"When are they meeting?"

"Tomorrow afternoon."

She went through her schedule. "I have a lesson from one to two."

"The team meets at three-thirty. Can you make it here by then?"

"I suppose." Did she really want to do this?

No, but if she planned on sticking around, she needed to show she was a team player. Maybe this was Mike's way of admitting her work had merit.

Or maybe it had something to do with what had happened between them.

Did she really want to ask him?

"Good. We'll be meeting in my office. If you ask at the information desk, they'll help you find it. See you tomorrow."

With that, he was gone. Shoving her cell phone into the back pocket of her jeans, she picked up her pitchfork and began cleaning the stalls again, forking up a clump of manure and depositing it into the wheelbarrow parked in the doorway of the stall.

This was actually Larry's job. The man's brows had lifted when he saw her scooping the waste from Brutus's straw, but he'd let her continue. She'd needed time to think this morning. No better way to do that than to engage in a mindless task that worked her muscles while letting her brain sort through various problems. Like why she'd washed her sheets this morning and had been sorely disappointed when Mike made no mention of coming out to the barn. Or the way her heart had pounded in her chest when she'd looked at the screen of her phone the second it rang and she saw his name displayed in large block letters.

Sex with Mike was wild and dangerous. He wasn't afraid to play a little bit rough, and she found she liked it, which was a revelation. A kind of scary one, in fact. Sex with Roger had been polished and sophisticated. She'd been fine with it at the time. Mike, however... Well as urbane as he might appear on the surface, or even on the phone a few minutes earlier, she'd glimpsed what the man was capable of. And oh was he capable.

Wrap your legs around me and get ready to hold on tight. Those growled word still had the power to make her insides turn moist and needy.

Sweat gathered on her brow as she hefted another scoop onto the growing pile. She stabbed the pitchfork into the heap and wiped her forehead with the back of her hand. She didn't want to leave Dusty Hills. She liked it here. She liked the people, loved her clients. But what if Mike kept digging or wanted the sheriff to ask a few more questions. The Feds had warned her about revealing anything, or letting anyone get too close to the truth.

She was supposed to call them immediately if things got out of hand.

So why wasn't she on the phone already? She should leave—knew it in her soul of souls, but she couldn't bring herself to make that call.

It wasn't because of Mike.

His face swam in her subconscious. The memory of what they'd done together on the porch.

Okay, it *was* because of him. The way he'd gone from angry to worried in the space of a few gasped breaths. The way he smiled at her. Murmured things no one had ever murmured to her in her life.

Lord. What was she doing? She was playing with fire, and she knew it. Falling in love with him would be an even bigger mistake than sleeping with him. She was already inches away and creeping closer by the second. But she couldn't seem to make herself stop, no matter what the cost.

If she wasn't careful, she might find that price suddenly skyrocketing to devastating proportions. And then who exactly would end up paying for the choices she made? Her?

Or Mike?

Trisha explained her theories with grace and skill, using the large pad and easel at the front of the conference room, while three of Mike's colleagues took notes. Bringing her here could very well be a mistake, but something in her face when she'd declared that she was the person he saw in front of him made him believe her. As had the way she'd twisted that class ring at the mention of marriage. She had been married at one time, he was pretty sure, but she didn't want him or anyone else to know.

Why?

The thought had struck him that whoever it was had done something to her. Something so awful she didn't want to discuss it. Or maybe it was that she didn't want her former husband finding her.

That made his hands draw up into tight fists as she talked about muscle memory and its importance in stimulating a damaged brain. Theories he knew from his own studies, but had never related to horses.

That she worked with them still made him uneasy, but that worry had calmed somewhat. Her animals were gentle enough to work with children. He'd been on one of them himself. There'd been no hint of the animal doing anything unexpected. And she wasn't a trainer by profession, so she wasn't working with untried or unruly mounts like Marcy had done on a regular basis. And Trisha had people helping her around the barn, while Marcy had preferred to train and ride when no one else was there—maybe to hide her affair from prying eyes. That habit had contributed to her death. There'd been no one around when the worst had happened. No one to hold her—not even her lover—as her higher brain function slowly receded into nothingness.

Swallowing, he leaned back in his chair just as Trisha swiveled toward them, her eyes finding his. A tiny frown puckered the smooth flesh between her brows, and he forced his own expression to slide back to neutral, afraid she'd seen some of his thoughts.

What was the big deal? They'd had sex a couple of times. He wasn't after a lasting relationship, and he got the feeling he wasn't the only one who wanted to keep it that way. She didn't deem it important that he know the truth about who she was, so why couldn't he just leave it at that? Her presentation this afternoon was proof that she knew what she was talking about. That's all he cared about. They could have a little fun together, keep things from getting too serious. A win/win situation, if ever he saw one.

So why did that plan create a sense of discomfort, like a pebble in a pair of running shoes that jabbed at his insole with each step he took? No matter which direction he went...no matter how fast or slow he went, it was still there.

Well, he could go for a pretty long time with that rock in his shoe before he finally had to reach down and get rid of it. He could deal with it later. In the meantime, she seemed to like sex with him—he definitely liked it with her.

No problemo, right?

Right.

In fact, the less he knew about her the better. If she wasn't spilling any deep dark secrets, it meant she didn't see him as permanent companionship material. Even better. He could keep his heart out of it, just like he had with the other two women he'd been with.

With that plan in mind, he settled in to listen to the rest of Trisha's presentation. And did a few quick calculations on what his next move should be.

Because he definitely wanted to make a move. Especially now that he was sure it was safe.

A half-hour later, though, he found himself heading for a veterinary clinic halfway across town. He'd asked if Trisha had had anything to eat, since it was after five. She hadn't—she'd been too busy getting her presentation together to do anything but work. Something that sent a stab of guilt through him. He hadn't given her much time to get ready, but then again, he hadn't given himself much time to prepare for seeing her again. His decision had been impulsive, needing to invent a reason to be around her.

Of course, she hadn't known that and had pulled together an impressive body of work that one of the other doctors had asked to be sent to him for future reference. And the man had leaned forward in his chair as he asked her a question or two, nodding as she'd answered him. Mike's spine had stiffened, and he'd given his colleague a measured glance, but had seen nothing in him but professional interest. Trisha had colored when another doctor had praised her for being so thorough. She had every right to be proud. She'd done a great job.

As soon as the room cleared out, he'd asked her out to dinner. She'd accepted. He didn't know whether to be thrilled or wary. He decided there was room for both.

Then she'd mentioned the vet visit.

"Laredo is due to be released today, and I want to make sure he trailers okay before they get to the ranch, since we'll be working with him as soon as Sarah is recovered and ready to ride again. I'll exercise him myself so he stays in shape."

"You won't work with him until you're sure it's safe, though, right?"

She glanced at him, then a funny expression passed across her face and was gone. "Nothing in life is ever perfectly safe."

He was being ridiculous. Trisha had never given any indication that she took safety for granted. All her students wore helmets. Hell, she'd made *him* wear a helmet when she put him on that stocky black horse. Marcy had grown up around horses, didn't feel the need to use them. His chest tightened.

The touch of her fingers on his arm had him looking at her again. "Mike, I promise I won't take unnecessary chances, okay? I just want to see his reaction to being loaded this first time. It might not be a problem. But if it is, I want to know it before I get into a situation that could put Sarah in danger."

His jaw relaxed again. She was being careful. Not taking unnecessary chances. He forced a note of unconcern in his voice. "Glad to hear it."

A thought came to him. Maybe if he told her about his wife, she'd take even more care. Why that was suddenly so important, he wasn't going to examine at the moment.

A man in a lab coat came out of the back. "Hey Trisha, you about ready to help us move that big boy?"

A knot formed in Mike's gut. Help? He'd thought they were just there to observe.

Trisha took her hand off his arm. "I want to stand back and watch his reactions, if that's okay?"

"Really? You've always insisted on being hands on with Brute Boy."

She shifted beside him and a beat or two passed. What was the problem?

"I only insist because he gets nervous around strangers."

"Nervous. That's one way to put it." The man shrugged. "Okay, so you're going to observe. Well, we've got him out back ready to see what happens. I'll call one of my other assistants to help."

Mike didn't want to be here. Didn't want to watch a jittery horse in action, putting everyone around it in danger, especially knowing that Trisha would normally have been right in the thick of things, if the vet's words were anything to go by. It was just another reminder of how his wife had died. Trisha had reassured him for a second or two, but this man's playful comments had brought his thoughts simmering back up where they frothed and circled like bubbles in a pan, waiting for the slightest increase in temperature to flare up and boil over.

They followed the vet to the back and Trisha murmured in a slow voice. "He's joking. I only help when I think it will put Brutus at ease."

So she only helped when the animal was agitated. Dangerous. Her words did nothing to calm him. Especially after hearing the vet refer to Brutus as Brute Boy. He'd done something to deserve that reputation.

Tell her about Marcy. Tonight. Over dinner.

They got to the back area of the clinic, where the horse—not as big as Crow or Brutus, with bones that looked finer—stood in a dirt yard, a horse trailer parked about fifty feet in front of it. There was already a man standing next to the animal, a rope attached to its halter. Even as they stood there, Laredo put his head down and snorted. He glanced at the people around the animal. No one seemed to pay much attention to the sound. Except him. He gritted his teeth and tried to push past the worry.

Another assistant came through the doors. With one person holding the rope, one person on the other side and one person beside the horse's right flank, the vet clucked to him. The animal tossed his head and pranced to the side as he eyed the trailer in front of him.

Wasn't going to happen.

The group tried again, this time the man with the rope jiggled it while the other two clucked to the animal, trying to get it to move forward. Still nothing.

Trisha touched his arm again. "I'll be right back."

His stomach lurched. He knew she'd end up rushing in there. But other than demand she stay next to him, he was powerless to stop her. She didn't owe him anything.

Moving over to a nearby bale of hay, she grabbed a handful and caught the vet's eye by waving it. The man nodded at her and said, "Back into the trailer and see if he'll follow you in."

Get in the trailer? She'd be trapped in there, if something happened. But these people were all professionals. Surely they wouldn't let her do something they weren't confident she could do.

Trisha moved to the horse's head and let him sniff the bunch of hay. He pulled a section off, munching as if he hadn't a care in the world. But when he reached for another mouthful, Trisha backed up a step. He stretched out his neck, only to find the food just out of reach again. Step went his left front foot. Then his right. Trisha moved the bundle back and forth, making it look enticing. The horse moved forward again, heading right for the darkened opening of the trailer. She glanced backward as she neared the vehicle, keeping up the movements with her hand. She went up the ramp until she was standing just inside the doorway.

Laredo hesitated, but Trisha crooned to him in a coaxing voice, "Come up and get it, boy. There's more inside." She moved back, until she was covered in shadow out of sight. The man with the rope handed it to Trisha who must have taken it, although he couldn't tell exactly what she was doing. The vet and the guy who was behind the horse moved out of the way when a feminine cluck came from inside the trailer. The horse moved up the ramp without hesitation, this time, and disappeared inside.

The men applauded, all except Mike whose whole being was focused on that trailer and the back opening. When Trisha appeared on the right side of the vehicle, he blinked in surprise until he noted another door at the front. So that's how they did it. She was soon at his side, looking up into his face.

"Hey, you okay?"

"Yep." A lie, but she didn't need to know that.

She smiled. "He did well, better than I thought he would."

Was she kidding? He'd had visions of the horse rearing, taking out several people as he struggled, not the least of them Trisha.

"I hate to think what 'bad' would have looked like."

Her smile faded. "We wouldn't have forced him into the trailer, if that's what you're thinking. It would only make things worse. We'd have given him more time. Gone slowly. Or given him something to calm him. But he didn't need it." She stepped closer. "Horses don't think like people do. He doesn't necessarily associate what happened to him with the trailer itself. And he wasn't trapped inside of the other one for long, we got him out pretty quickly and on his feet."

Mike reached out and touched her cheek. She believed what she was saying. It was there in those beautiful green eyes, which closed at his touch, leaning into his fingers.

"Trisha?" The vet's voice broke in, breaking the spell between them. "You want us to drive Laredo right back to your place?"

"Do you mind?" Trisha moved a few feet away. "Larry is at the barn, he's expecting you. I don't think Laredo will give you any problems unloading."

The vet glanced inside the trailer, where the horse was still chewing a mouthful of hay. "He's more interested in eating than in what's going on around him, so I think we're good." The other man met Mike's eye. "Are you two off?"

Mike answered before Trisha could. "We're headed out to get a bite to eat."

Admitting they were doing it together surprised him,

but he held the vet's gaze without blinking. The other man nodded. "Choose somewhere good. She's worth it."

Trisha stepped next to the vet and kissed the guy's cheek. "Thanks. Take care of Laredo for me."

"Will do. Take care of yourself." With one last look at Mike, the vet turned around and headed back for the trailer. That left him alone with Trisha, and an aching sense that like Laredo and his obsession with his hay, Mike was far too interested in the woman in front of him to notice anything else around him. Like the fact that he was falling for her, despite his best efforts. And between her profession and whatever deep dark secret she was harboring, it made the prospect of falling in love with her dangerous on a whole lot of levels.

CHAPTER ELEVEN

"THE TEAM WAS impressed with your presentation."

Trisha glanced up from her plate of chicken fried steak as the low words hung between them. With the bite of meat still on her fork, she couldn't help but stare for a second or two. She'd been trying to convince him of the merits of hippotherapy from their first meeting so this hundred-and-eighty-degree turn seemed a bit sudden. Wait. He'd said the *team* was impressed, not him. "How could you tell?"

He quirked one side of his mouth in a rueful grin. "By the amount of notes they were taking. I've never seen them scribbling so fast. And I'm supposed to be the team leader on this particular case."

"It's just something new for them. Not because what I do is anything special."

"I'm beginning to think it is. Very special."

Wow. Maybe he *was* including himself in that impressed bunch. The thought was heady, making her insides do a quick twirl before settling back into place. "Thank you, Mike. That means a lot to me. Especially since I know you're not overly fond of horses."

"It's not that I'm not fond of them. It's that..." He waved away whatever he'd been going to say and picked up his glass of iced tea, taking a hefty sip and making her wonder if he was about to mention his late wife. "I was surprised you'd want to come to a mom and pop joint like Aunt Sadie's. We do have a couple of nice places in Mariston that serve sushi or some such."

The slight look of distaste on his face at the word "sushi' made her forget about her curiosity over his wife's death. She grinned instead. "Believe me, I've had enough sushi to last me a lifetime. But I've never really gotten to eat in a place like this." She glanced around the interior of the simple diner that served massive portions of country-fried steak, chicken, pork, liver…well, just about anything that could be battered and fried.

"Really? I'd think with the amount of traveling you did as a kid, you'd have eaten in a greasy spoon a time or two in your life." His eyes had turned sharp and watchful.

Crap. Being with Mike made her forget she should be pretending to be something she wasn't: a military brat who'd lived in a thousand different places. Not the New York City native she was, who'd eaten sushi, caviar, and other exotic dishes during her marriage to Roger.

She averted her eyes and cursed herself for having to lie yet again. But it was for his own good. And for hers. "My mom was picky about where she ate. She liked nice restaurants."

"I see." But he didn't. She could see it in his eyes—a kind of disappointment that went beyond types of food and childhood backgrounds. He knew she was making this up as she went, and it hurt much more than it should have to keep up the ruse. Maybe she could tell him. Maybe she could ask him to promise to keep it a secret. He'd kept their little rendezvous on the porch quiet, as far as she could tell.

But the sheriff was going to want to know if Mike had

talked to her. What she'd said. He was a law enforcement officer first. Mike would have to lie to avoid telling the truth. Did she really want to make him an accessory? He was an honest, hard-working man. A good man. He had integrity. Cared deeply about his patients. No, he hadn't volunteered information about his wife, but why would he? It was none of her business. And his wife's death didn't call into question his credibility as a neuro-surgeon. Her falsified background, however, would make any doctor in his right mind ask some hard questions and expect straight answers. Answers she couldn't give.

Unless…she told him.

You can't, Trisha. This isn't just about your safety. It's about Mike's…your mom's, your brother's. And what about her contacts with the Feds? She'd already watched one of them die right in front of her. Would her careless-ness endanger others? Or would it encourage the bad guys to keep looking for ways to compromise the pro-gram…make people to afraid to testify, if something happened to her or someone close to her?

To keep herself from temptation, she finally popped the bite of steak into her mouth and forced herself to chew. It was cold now, though, and pretty much tasted like cardboard, a far different reaction than she'd had a few minutes ago.

Plastering a smile on her face that felt as fake as her whole screwed-up life, she kept up a stream of small talk in between bites of food. When her mouth wasn't chew-ing, it was spilling out a load of nonsense. She figured if she controlled the conversation, he couldn't ask her any other questions. Questions that might require less than honest answers. Because the last thing Trisha wanted to do was lie to this man any more than she already had. So she talked, and talked, and talked.

They headed out to the car as soon as the meal was over, and she kept on ripping through subjects that ranged from diseases of a horse's hooves to the most effective composting methods for manure. Fitting really, since she seemed to be shoveling the stuff as fast as she could.

Mike opened the car door for her just as a middle-aged woman, hair in a bun, appeared at the entrance to the restaurant, waving frantically. "Dr. Mike, I hate to call you back, but Reginald has done some kind of fool thing to his arm. He's bleeding bad."

Trisha's stomach turned over, a familiar queasiness creeping up her throat.

"Stay here," Mike said, leaving the car door open as he swung back toward the restaurant and hurried to the woman, asking for details as he went.

As much as she hated blood, Mike might need her help if it was something serious, so she slammed the door and went after the pair, catching up with them in the entry-way. He threw her a glance that held the merest hint of a frown but didn't try to order her back to the car.

As if that would work.

"He's in the kitchen. He wanted to just wrap it with a bandage, but it bled right through, and he refuses to go to the hospital."

Mike's steps quickened, his long strides eating up the distance through the dining area, where several patrons were on their feet. She soon heard why. The sounds of profanity and threats reached her ears at about the same time as her companion pushed through the double doors that led to the diner's food-prep area.

Her eyes went wide when she saw a crimson arc that covered a six-foot section of white tile floor. Blood. The shouting continued as an older man in a white T-shirt and matching slacks held his arm over the sink, a dark red cloth wrapped around and around it. Trisha didn't think bandages came in fashion colors, which meant that had to be…more blood. Especially since the bandage was dripping the same-colored substance into the large stainless-steel sink. The hand holding the bandage in place was also dripping blood.

"Oh, no."

The nausea in her throat sloshed higher, but she forced it back with a swallow.

Mike didn't waste any time. "Call 911 and tell them to get an ambulance out here." Moving next to the man, he took hold of the arm, despite Reginald trying to jerk it away again.

"It's just a little cut. Sadie, why'd you have to call him back here?"

The woman snapped back a curt response.

Mike cut through the squabbling. "What happened?"

"The knife drawer got stuck, and I reached in to see if something was blocking it." Reginald glared around them. "Who was the idiot who put a knife in the drawer cutting side up?"

Trisha cringed as she remembered exactly how much force was required to puncture human skin and how it had felt to have hot blood spill over her hand as she'd pulled free of her attacker. Mike glanced back at her, unaware of her internal struggles. "You up to helping?"

She would have to be. This man's life was at stake. "Yes."

He started quickly unwrapping the bandage, still ignoring Reginald's ranting. Trisha crossed over to him, blocking out everything except Mike's face and the sound of his voice. "As soon as I get this off, I need to find out whether we're dealing with a vein or an artery and apply pressure."

"Just tell me what to do."

The bandage fell away and a bright red stream of blood spurted into the sink from a large gash on the man's inner arm, near his elbow. Mike quickly pressed his thumb to an area just above the injury, muttering an oath of his own. The blood flow slowed, but didn't stop completely. Trisha didn't know the difference between a vein and an artery, but she had a feeling from Mike's reaction that it was the worst option of the two. He glanced up at Sadie, the lines of his face hard and tight. "I need a couple of cloth napkins, preferably ones that have just come out of the dryer, they'll be cleaner."

"Right away, Dr. Mike." The woman hurried to do as he'd asked. The other three employees stood back, their faces various shades of green and gray. Mike asked them to go out and see if they could clear out the restaurant and watch for the ambulance. She had a feeling the suggestion had more to do with getting them out of the kitchen than anything else. The injured man was looking a little ill himself, pale faced, bracing his arms on the edges of the sink now to hold himself up.

She remembered Roger screaming at her, clutching his side as he'd backed away from her...the way she'd gasped in a couple of breaths and had rolled off the desk, gripping the bloodstained letter opener between shaking fingers, ready to strike again if need be. Her hand went to her stomach.

"Trisha!" Mike's voice yanked her back to the situation at hand. "I need you to grab a couple of pairs of gloves from that box over on the counter. A pair for me and a pair for you." She glanced over to where he was looking and saw a large cardboard box with the words "Gloves for Food Handlers" written on the side. Hurrying over, she ripped four gloves from the inside and spied a pump bottle of hand sanitizer next to it. She squirted some onto her hands and rubbed them together before donning one pair of gloves. She carried the bottle and the other pair to Mike, glad to have something to do.

"Perfect."

Reginald was no longer swearing. He was sweating, despite the chill of the air-conditioner, and his arm was still dripping blood at a steady rate. But at least it wasn't shooting into the sink any more. "What do you want me to do?"

"I'm going to need you to put your thumb just behind mine and press as hard as you can, so I can get my gloves on, okay?"

Trisha gulped. "Okay."

Just as she set the gloves and sanitizer on a clean section of counter, Sadie arrived with a handful of white napkins.

"Thanks," he said.

She could do this. She could.

Sliding next to him, she placed her gloved thumb on the spot on the man's arm, just behind where Mike's was.

"Harder," he said.

Huffing in a quick breath, she pressed down with all her might, wrapping her fingers beneath the man's arm for more leverage. "Like that?"

"Yes. Now hold it." With that, he released his grip. Trisha's own pulse pounded in her ears when she realized that if she let go, Reginald could bleed to death.

Where was that ambulance?

Mike sanitized his hands, then took two of the napkins from Sadie and tied the ends together to form a longer length of cloth. She was surprised he hadn't just ripped off his belt and used it as a tourniquet, like you saw on television. He knew what he was doing, though.

He'd pressed on exactly the right spot to get the bleeding to slow down.

Her hand was starting to cramp from holding on so tight and she'd only been here for a minute or two. Still, she held on.

He shoved his hands into his gloves and grabbed the napkin again. "You okay?" he asked her.

"Yes." She'd keep the pressure on no matter how long it took.

Mike took the tied napkins and looped them around the man's arm, lining up the place he'd knotted with the spot he'd held earlier. Then he tied it tight. "The knot should press on the artery until the ambulance gets here." He nodded at her. "Release some of the pressure and see if it works."

Sadie's voice came from behind them. "He'll be okay, won't he?"

"He's going to be fine."

In the distance, Trisha could hear the tell-tale shriek of a siren.

Finally.

Mike tapped her thumb. "Take off some of the pressure."

She hesitated, then eased her thumb back slowly, braced to press again if the blood flowed too fast. Nothing happened. The wound still dripped, but it wasn't gushing.

The sound of the siren grew to ear-shattering levels and then abruptly shut off.

Trisha had avoided looking at the gash until now, but she could see it was ugly, the cut deep and clean, the surrounding skin stained dark with blood. She was no doctor, but she was pretty sure he'd need surgery to repair the damage.

The rattle of a gurney behind her signaled the presence of the EMS team, and she took a couple of quick steps back so they could get to the man. Mike stayed where he was, giving the two men in blue uniforms a rundown on what they had and what he wanted done.

Wow. The man really did like being in charge. Then again, he *was* the doctor, and he'd probably just saved Reginald's life.

The two emergency services workers obviously knew who Mike was, because they treated him with a kind of awed deference as they jumped to do what he asked, taking Reginald's vitals, hooking him up to an IV and getting him on the gurney. They ignored their patient's muttered threats, just like Mike had, although the tirade was much less vehement now than it had been earlier, as the man realized how serious his situation was.

When the emergency technicians whisked the gurney out of the kitchen toward the waiting ambulance, with Sadie trotting alongside it, she was surprised when Mike hung back. Especially after the way he'd directed the treatment. "Aren't you going with them to the hospital?"

"No, I'll just be in the way at this point. Stu and Gary know what they're doing."

So he did know them. Not surprising, since he'd probably worked with a lot of the local ambulance services. And he evidently could give up control when he trusted the other party to do their job.

Like when he'd ridden Crow, his hands braced on those strong thighs? Had he trusted her to do her job?

Not the time, Trisha.

Mike stripped his gloves off and nodded that she could do the same, while he explained to the restaurant staff that they'd need to close the place for at least the rest of the day. He asked for volunteers to stay and help clean up. Not surprisingly, every hand went up. Mike really did have an impressive array of talents.

As they walked through the door, he gave a soft chuckle. "Not exactly the way I envisioned spending our time after dinner."

He'd thought about them spending more time together after dinner? Doing what?

Mike opened the car door for her and she slid in, her breath sticking in her lungs as he went around to the other side and climbed behind the wheel. Had he been thinking about that promised horizontal? For some reason, the thought of having him on a bed, pressing her into the mattress, seemed even more intimate than what they'd already done, if that was possible. It was better not to jump to conclusions, however. Maybe he just meant to take her straight home, drop her off, and then be on his way.

Fifteen minutes later she had her answer when he turned into the long driveway that led to her house.

"Anyone here besides the horses?" he asked when he pulled to a halt. Neither Penny nor Larry's vehicles were there, and there was no sign of the vet's trailer, so Laredo had already been settled into his stall for the evening.

"No." She wanted to ask him in. Wanted to cash in that rain check, but what if she was wrong? What if the last thing on his mind after having to treat an unexpected emergency was sex?

It shouldn't even be on *her* mind, but it was. They'd saved a life. Both of them. They'd worked together, and she'd faced down her memories without passing out. Thanks to Mike.

It was exhilarating. Life-affirming. And she wanted to celebrate it. In Mike's arms, no matter how stupid or unwise that might be. The world hadn't collapsed the last two times they'd been together, so it probably wouldn't fall apart this time either.

If she was worried about being pressed against him skin to skin, limbs entwined together as they made love, maybe she could figure out a way to get what she wanted while not giving up too much of herself in the process.

Hmm...what if, like on Crow, he let her call the shots for once. She could just put him in a chair and lower herself...

She gulped, just thinking about it.

Still, what if he didn't want her? She threaded her fingers through each other and squeezed them together. Should she just open the door and get out?

Her hand went to the latch then Mike's low, gravelly tones swirled through the shadows in the car. "Are you going to ask me in?"

"Do you *want* to come in? F-for coffee, I mean?"

He reached across and gently gripped her chin, turning her toward him. "I want to come in," he confirmed. "But not for coffee."

No coffee! That meant...

She smiled and leaned back in her seat, the tension draining out of her shoulders. "I'm all out of coffee anyway."

Returning her grin, he leaned over and dropped a kiss on her mouth, letting it linger for a second or two. Her pulse rate shot up, punching a hole right through the roof of the car and galloping away.

"Good thing I'm not here for the coffee, then, isn't it?"

With that, the door clicked open and Mike Dunning, his intentions plain for all to see, got out of the car and circled the hood. When he reached a hand out to her, she allowed him to help her from the vehicle, her legs trembling harder than they had during the rescue efforts at the restaurant.

As if he knew she was in danger of sinking to the ground in a heap, he swept her into his arms and started toward her front porch, where he took the four wooden steps with an ease that made her mouth water. "Well, Ms. Bolton, now that I have you back in my clutches, I think it's time I fulfill a certain promise."

CHAPTER TWELVE

STILL HOLDING HER in his arms, Mike waited for her to unlock her front door before pushing through it and leaning against it to close it.

"Horizontal surface?" He glanced around, spying a plush beige sofa with a large cushioned ottoman in front of it—both horizontal. A little further in there was a long plank farm table that made his mouth water—also horizontal.

Hmm…countertops. He didn't remember promising *he'd* be horizontal. She could sprawl out on that dining room table—all curves and hollows readily available, while he remained standing, sampling, licking… And, yep, there went his body, right on cue.

Trisha bit her lip then looped her arms around his neck. "I know you want to wind up flat on your back." She raised a brow at him when he started to protest. "You said 'horizontal,' but you never mentioned who exactly was going to be on top."

"Me." He tightened his fingers around her.

"You have a hard time giving up control, don't you?"

Was she kidding him? The last two times they'd been together he'd hung onto his control by a thread. Which was why he wanted to be in the driver's seat. "That's me. Mr. Control Freak."

She laughed. "I think you are, actually. I only know of one time that you relinquished that control. When you were sitting on Crow."

And what exactly did that horse have to do with anything? "I'm not following you."

"Easy. I think it's time for lesson number two."

Now? Hardly. "I think you've misread my intentions." He cocked his head. "Although I get the feeling that might be deliberate."

"I know exactly what you want." She slid a hand into the thick hair at the back of his head and curled her fingers around it, tightening just enough to let his scalp know she was there. Then she tugged, forcing his head back an inch before she leaned forward and ran her tongue up the side of his neck.

He almost dropped her, his fingers going boneless as a wave of pure pleasure sloshed into his gut. "Trisha."

She was at his ear now. "Give up a little of that control, Doctor. I'll make it worth your while. Promise." She nipped his earlobe. "You let me call the shots once. I know you can do it again."

That was the whole problem. He wouldn't be able to *do it* again. At least not right away. But the thought of what she might do if he handed her the reins made all the synapses in his brain start firing at once. Suddenly he wanted it. Wanted to see her lean over him as she lowered herself onto him. He could lie on the bed and watch each change of expression on that lovely face.

He kissed the thought of the dining-room table goodbye. At least for now.

Did it matter that he still knew practically nothing about her? Yes, it did. Did it matter right this second? Hell, no.

"Okay," he agreed. "Lesson number two. Where's your bedroom?"

"I was thinking dining room."

The table swung back into his line of sight. Sounded good to him. More than good, actually. He started toward it, while she held on. When they reached the table he set her down on it, only to have her slide off and pull one of the chairs out, turning it so that the seat faced out. Then she sat, slowly, and his heart ricocheted around in his chest cavity for a few seconds when she reached out and grabbed the fabric of his slacks and urged him toward her.

Wow.

She undid his belt buckle. Then her nimble fingers went to the button on his pants and released it, followed by the quick snick of his zipper going down. "Remember when you were on Crow and I asked you to put your hands on your thighs and leave them there?"

Did he remember? His brain wasn't quite firing correctly at the moment, but somehow he managed to bite out "Yes" in response.

"In a minute I'm going to switch places with you and you're going to do that again." Her palms traveled around his hips and smoothed over his butt, giving a quick squeeze that had him tensing up. "Do you have something in this wallet?"

She eased it from his pocket and held it up.

"In one of the pockets on the right-hand side."

Leaving him standing there for a second, she flipped it open, hesitating for a second as she looked at something he couldn't see, then found the condom, plucking it from its hiding place. He briefly wondered what she'd looked at. She flicked the wallet onto the table and set the condom down next to it.

All thoughts of that fled when she reached for him again, tucking her fingers into the waistband of his pants and tugging them and his briefs down with one quick pull. Then he was bare, and there was the evidence that this woman affected him in a million different ways. He was so hard he could feel the blood pulsing in time with his heartbeat.

Trisha scooted forward on her chair, parting her legs so that her thighs were on either side of his knees.

And her mouth…

Her mouth was millimeters from the head of his erection. So close that the warmth of her breath washed over him each time she exhaled.

Her eyes flickered up to his. "Do you want me to?"

He didn't need to ask what she meant. Instead, a million different responses flooded his head: *Yes. No. Not yet. Please.*

None of them made it past his lips.

She smiled and wrapped a hand around him, sliding it all the way to the base. "I think we'll leave this until a little later." Then she let go and stood, the heady sensation of her body scraping slowly up his swollen flesh making him hiss in a breath and hold it until she was all the way up, pressed tight against him, feet still splayed on either side of his.

Her head tipped back. "Ready?"

She gripped his arms and pivoted, turning them both until his back was to the chair. "Now sit."

The command was softened with another smile, but her hands went to his shoulders and pushed. And hell if his legs didn't bend immediately, until his naked butt was parked on the chair, slacks and briefs around his ankles.

She knelt and took care of that, pulling them the rest of the way off and draping them over another chair.

He knew Trisha had a bossy streak, but this was unbelievably erotic, having her manipulate him, using her hands and voice to tell him exactly what she wanted him to do.

And he was going to do it. All of it. If she could play, then so could he. In fact, this game might just become one of his favorites.

She stood again. "Okay, Doctor, hands on your thighs, just like you did with Crow. Only this time you won't be riding him." Her lips curved in a saucy look that was pure sex. "In fact, you won't be the one doing the riding at all."

His flesh jerked at that thought.

As if she knew exactly what he was thinking, she parted her legs and moved to stand over his knees, putting her hips just at eye level. All he wanted to do was reach out and grab them and yank her closer. His palms went to the backs of her thighs, and she immediately took a step back, brows up. "Uh-uh, Mike. Not allowed. Hands on your own thighs."

Gritting his teeth in frustration, he did as she asked. She was right. He liked control. Because right now all he wanted to do was grab the woman, toss her onto that table beside them and thrust into her hard and deep.

He fought back the impulse. She wanted this, so who was he to take that from her?

Planting his hands on his legs, he waited for her to move back into place. It killed him to sit here like a lump when everything in him wanted to touch…to taste…to possess.

As soon as Trisha had stepped forward again, she set her hands on his shoulders and slowly lowered herself until she was sitting on his legs, her thighs resting on top of his hands. He couldn't move them now, even if he wanted to. Maybe that's what she had in mind.

She leaned in and kissed him. He wanted to bury his fingers in her hair and hold her in place, but of course he couldn't. Instead, she molded her hands to his head, her lips playing peek-a-boo with his, light touches that aroused him to a fever pitch but didn't satisfy.

Using her own hands as leverage, he pressed his mouth hard to hers, his lips parting hers and holding them wide open as he plunged his tongue deep into her.

Yes! This!

She didn't push him away this time, just pulled him closer and let him do exactly to her mouth what he planned on doing to her body as soon as his hands were free. She was right. He wanted control, and if he couldn't get it one way, he was going to get it another.

A minute later she hauled herself up and off his lap, tearing her mouth from his. Breathing heavily, she pressed the back of her hand to her lips, looking a little less sure of herself than she had a second ago. She stared at him as if seeing him for the first time, then her eyes lowered to his lap and came back up. He watched her swallow.

He was more than ready to find that horizontal surface.

"Ready to hand the reins back?" One eyebrow cocked, daring her to say she hadn't liked what he'd just done.

"I..." She blinked a couple of times then seemed to pull herself back together. "No. Not yet."

Her fingers went to the bottom of her T-shirt and hauled the thing up and over her head. His throat dried up. "Not yet," she repeated, her voice firming up again. "I want you to sit right there while I take my clothes off, one piece at a time."

He'd almost made her lose her place. Almost made her give in and let him carry her off to her bedroom. His kiss had made her crave him in a way that she never would have dreamed possible six months ago.

That's what had knocked her back to reality...and back to her plan. She wanted him—merciful heavens, she wanted him—but it had to be on her terms or she was lost.

Keep up the saucy act, Trisha. Men are supposed to love it when women take over and drive them wild. Right? So why did Mike make it seem like torture? Like he wanted nothing more than to pin her arms over her head and take her?

She was the one being tortured. She wanted him to rip all her clothes off and have his wicked way with her.

Unzipping her pants, she forced her eyes to stay steady on his. At least one of his body parts wasn't complaining about what she was doing. That part stood hard and firm, willing her to get down there and pay it some attention.

Oh, she would. Very soon. Then he would forget all about her bed. They'd stay right here and make love on that chair. And they would both get what they wanted, of that Trisha would make sure.

Off came her pants. And then her bra.

"Come here."

His voice was soft. Coaxing. And she wanted nothing more than to do its bidding.

"When I'm ready." She hooked her thumbs in the waistband of her black bikini panties, noting that his fingers were now digging into the flesh of his thighs, as if forcing them to remain in place.

Her panties slid over her hips and down her thighs before she stepped out of them.

"Let go of the reins, Trisha."

Soon. She just needed him too far gone before handing them over. "Not yet."

Up came his eyes, pupils so large they threatened to

swallow her whole. "You are going to be sorry you ever ventured down this particular road, woman. Because two can play at this game. And believe me when I say you are going to remember this night. Every time you sit on one of those horses, every time you slide into your bed, you are going to feel me. Right. There."

Her lips parted, her heart hammering in her chest as something deep and profound swept through her, a heat blooming in her belly and encasing her heart. She wanted him. Wanted him on his terms. Wanted him however she could get him.

She opened her hand, a symbolic gesture that meant nothing and everything. "Take them."

He didn't hesitate, coming off the chair and grabbing her up into his arms, his lips coming down onto hers and taking them. On his terms. Needy. Powerful. This time she didn't try to get away, just let him have his fill, finding herself burying her fingers into his hair and trying to force their mouths even closer.

When he finally lifted his head, she had to keep holding on to prevent herself from falling down. He kicked off his shoes, and reached over to snatch up the condom. "Bed. Now."

"Okay."

What else could she say? If he didn't take her soon, she might actually explode into a thousand pieces right here in the living room…before he even touched her. She was in danger of it even now.

He hauled his shirt over his head, baring his shoulders and torso. Not that he gave her much time to admire him because he had her by the hand, dragging her with him as he strode down the hallway and led her toward her own personal version of ecstasy…and agony.

* * *

Trisha slowly pushed her way toward the light, eyes cracking open enough to realize the light wasn't just in her imagination. It was all around her. Morning. She rolled onto her back, groaning as a languid soreness flowed through each bundle of muscles.

He hadn't been kidding. She was going to remember last night for the next several days.

Even as she thought it, her nipples tightened, remembered pleasure washing over her.

When she'd handed over the reins, he'd taken them and showed her what real control was all about. And that man was the master of his own body...and hers.

Lordy!

Flinging her hand to the side, she was disappointed when it landed on cool sheets instead of a warm, firm body. He'd left? Without saying goodbye?

She sat up with a frown then heard the sounds of water running in the adjoining bathroom. Okay, he was in the shower.

And he hadn't asked her about her past. Not once. Not before, during or after their lovemaking session. A renewed sense of hope swept through her. Yes, being in bed with him had been incredibly intimate, but it had also been freeing. And wonderful. Maybe things weren't as dire as she'd made them out to be.

After all, Dusty Hills was kind of in its own little bubble. They had contact with other towns, but the residents all knew and cared about each other...in fact, most of them had been born and raised here, except for a few outsiders who'd married residents of Dusty Hills and had come back to live with that person. It wasn't like any of them knew people from New York City or were likely to travel there and blab about the stranger who'd moved to their town. She had a pretty solid identity—well, maybe the sheriff had seen some holes but he'd evidently not gone digging any further. And Mike seemed okay with letting go of the subject.

Visions of her and Mike doing a lot more of the stuff they'd done last night danced round and round like a music-box figure that never stopped. Why couldn't she have a normal life? Find someone to love…

She swallowed. Find someone to love. Mike?

It would seem so.

But did he feel the same way? He'd never said anything about it, but the way he'd touched her…it had been personal. Much more personal than Roger's practiced lovemaking, which had been why she'd been so leery of winding up in bed with Mike. But it had been fine. More than fine.

The world hadn't ended. Neither had it paused for even a brief second when their bodies had finally tangled together in a heady mixture of tender lovemaking and wild sex that had made her cry out more than once.

She slid her feet off the bed and shrugged into an over-sized T-shirt, letting it slide off one of her shoulders. Maybe she could intercept him in the shower and have a little more of that together time.

Padding to the door, she tested the handle and found it unlocked. She entered the space on silent feet, hoping to surprise him. The steamy bathroom smelled of raspberry shampoo, which made her smile. He was evidently secure enough in his masculinity that he didn't mind using her frou-frou bath products.

She took off her earrings and her class ring, something she'd forgotten to do last night, and quickly brushed her teeth. Before she could finish, the water was switched off and in a panic she turned to see him emerge from her minuscule shower stall, a towel wrapped around his waist.

He smiled. "I didn't realize you were in here or I would have waited."

With the toothbrush dangling from her mouth and a glob of foam swirling around her tongue, she stared at him. For a neurosurgeon, he was surprisingly firm, the hint of muscles playing beneath the skin of his chest, the curve of biceps as he tucked the ends of his towel in around his waist. Long, lean fingers that could...

She turned and spit as gracefully as she could manage into the sink and turned on the water to rinse the residue down the drain. A pair of strong arms curled around her waist, and his chin came to rest on her bare shoulder. He smelled heavenly—of her soap, shampoo and a warm earthy musk that marked him as Mike Dunning...super-stud.

"I was trying to surprise you."

"Hmm." His teeth nipped where his chin had rested. "You've been just full of surprises over the last eight hours or so."

Her face heated. Only because he gave her sexuality a shot of confidence every time he laid those heated brown eyes on her.

Curling her right hand around the back of his neck to hold him against her, she used her other hand to toss her toothbrush back into the holder next to the sink. The fan in the bathroom had made short work of the steam, clearing the mirror and giving her a good view of him. He frowned for a second and then his hand reached out to capture her left one, his thumb sliding over her ring finger.

Her breath caught in her throat as he explored the naked skin, praying he wouldn't notice that there were two different indentations there. A wide strip from the class ring she now wore, but beneath it a deeper, narrower furrow, gouged out by a too-tight wedding band. The rasp of his skin against hers sent a shiver over her, and she glanced in the mirror, to find him studying her hand.

Please, don't ask. Not now.

He let go of her and looped his arms back around her middle, regarding her in the reflection with an expression that was both soft and sad. About her ring? No, she didn't think so. That had been curiosity, but to his credit he hadn't asked. She relaxed again.

"What is it?" she asked.

"I was married once. To a horse trainer."

Her stomach knotted into a tight ball that became more and more dense. She'd wanted to know. But suddenly she was terrified of him saying another word. She had no choice, though, unless she asked him to stop.

"Marcy died four years ago in a riding accident. The horse she was on was her favorite, one she had raised from a colt and trained herself."

"I'm so sorry, Mike."

He tightened his grip. "I wanted you to know why I'm so wary around horses....and women." Dropping a kiss on her shoulder, he went on. "I found out after her death she was having an affair...had lied repeatedly about where she was going and who she was with. It was like I didn't even know her at the end."

A heavy load of guilt settled on Trisha's shoulders. She'd lied to Mike too. Time and time again.

"Anyway, she was going into the outdoor arena and her horse evidently spooked—they found a dead rattler a few feet away. Marcy hit her head, breaking a vertebra in her neck. There was no hope. No brain activity. She was kept alive on machines for three days before her parents and I made the decision to donate her organs." His voice turned to rough gravel that ground her soul and made her eyes prick with tears. "I'm a neurosurgeon—went to school for twelve damn years—and I couldn't help my own wife."

Twisting round in his arms, Trisha pressed her cheek against his skin, hearing the fierce beating of his heart, drawing his warm scent deep into her lungs. This man had known such pain. Such betrayal. How could his wife have cheated on him? "You loved her, despite what she did."

"Yes. Very much. But it's also made me a wary man." His fingers came up to stroke her hair. They trailed along her left arm, following the line to where her hand lay flat against his chest. His thumb brushed over her ring finger, tracing just above the joint...the circle where her ring had lain. Just like he'd done earlier.

A chill went over her. That's why he was confiding in her. He wanted her to do the same. To tell him the truth about who she was. To prove she wouldn't hurt him the way his wife had.

She couldn't give him what he wanted. Not now. Not five years from now. Probably not ever.

Right on cue, a strange sense of expectancy began building in the air as he waited for her response.

That's what relationships were all about: sharing confidences; growing together through past experiences; being honest with each other. She'd hoped he'd be content to just be with her without any of that.

Maybe he still would. Maybe she'd give him silence as an answer, and he'd accept it as enough.

She took a step back, pulling her hand away and letting it drop to the counter next to her hip. Then she poured all the sincerity she could muster into her next words. "I'm sorry, Mike. So sorry. About everything."

Sorry she couldn't tell him the truth. Sorry she couldn't share key aspects of her life with him. Sorry that everything with her seemed to be one-sided, with Mike giving so much more than she ever could.

He could live in the light while she was forced to lurk in the shadows, a place where truth and fiction merged into an image that made her insides twist and numbed all but the most basic emotions.

Still, maybe that would be enough for him.

He studied her for a few seconds, a muscle working in his jaw. Then his eyes slowly slid back to her finger. And she knew it wouldn't be. He wouldn't stop until he knew the truth. Until he'd unmasked her and laid her bare.

She'd said she didn't want him in danger. Had wanted to draw a line in the sand and stay on her side of it. Did she really want to drag him over it and make him a part of her world? Make him lose sleep at night, wondering when her past would catch up to both of them?

No. She stuck her toe in the sand and redrew that line…deeper this time, keeping it firmly between her and Mike. She knew what she had to do.

Taking a deep breath and trying to ignore the pain in her heart, she chose her words carefully. "Thank you for last night. I had a good time."

A frown appeared. Not the response he'd expected. "So did I."

"I need to get out to the barn and start my day. The horses will be hungry." It was the only way she could think of to get him out of the house. No need to tell him that Larry normally did the morning chores. In fact, her barn helper was probably already out there.

His glance tracked over her loose shirt and bare legs.

Right. It was obvious she was dressed for a day at the barn, especially since she'd come into the bathroom to find him. She tried again. "I'll shower first, of course."

"Of course."

She slid out from between him and the counter, reaching for her class ring and screwing it back onto her finger—covering the truth with a lie. She faced him and waited, praying he wouldn't try to kiss her, because she'd do one of two things: burst into tears, or cling to him and never let him go.

Neither of those things would help her find the courage to take the next step. The only step. The Feds had said it would only take a single phone call.

Mike's jaw tightened, but he nodded. "I'll see myself out, then."

"Thanks."

As the bathroom door clicked behind him, she leaned her butt against the counter and closed her eyes.

One step at a time, Trisha. That's all you can do.

Even if those steps would carry her far away from Dusty Hills, Nevada. Far away from a man who, despite her best efforts, she now loved with all her heart.

CHAPTER THIRTEEN

"IT'LL TAKE US a week or so to iron out the details. Do you want to sit tight? Safe houses are reserved for worst-case scenarios. Unless there's something you're not telling us." Clyde, her FBI contact, didn't sound irritated. Or even flustered. It was as if this was all in a day's work for him.

Well, for him, maybe it was. But for her, it was her life. Her family's lives.

Pressing the phone to her ear, she contemplated her little piece of earth. How many times would she need to do this?

She wouldn't be doing it this time if she'd kept her heart under control. She'd have to be more careful in the future.

That was something she wouldn't have to worry about for a long, long time. She had a feeling her heart would still be feeling these wounds next month and the one after that. Maybe even for years.

"No, it's nothing urgent. Someone asked the sheriff to look into my past, and I don't think he's going to let it go."

"You want me to put in a friendly call to this sheriff and explain a thing or two to him? Let him know his questions are not welcomed?"

Leave it to Clyde to give the word "friendly' a sinister

edge. He'd never blamed her for his colleague's death. Not once. In fact, he'd assured her that any one of them would have willingly taken that bullet. It came with the job. Maybe so, but that didn't make it any easier to accept. Someone had died trying to protect her. She vowed she would never again be the reason someone got hurt.

"No, I think that'll just make it worse. This is small-town Nevada after all."

This time her contact laughed. "You were the one who chose the venue."

Yes, she was. So she had no one to blame but herself. "I think I'll let you guys choose this time, how's that sound?"

"I've got a few ideas. You up for some cold weather?"

Trisha could almost see the man's smile. With an attitude that matched the bristly gray hairs sprouting from his head, Clyde seemed to have developed a soft spot for her. She wasn't sure that was a good thing. The man was almost scarier than her ex.

"As long as it's somewhere my horses can live comfortably, it'll be perfect."

There was a brief moment of silence. Then he came back. "Those animals are a liability. We can't be responsible if—"

"I've already heard the spiel." How someone might be able to track her through her movements with the horse trailer. "The horses come with me. It was my one condition for testifying."

"Let's stick to approved language, okay?" This time there was a thread of irritation running through his voice.

Right. She'd forgotten. The wrong word to the wrong person could prove deadly, something that had been drilled into her head. She'd followed those rules to a *T* and look where that had gotten her. "Sorry. You'll call before you come?"

"Yes. Just remember that each contact carries a risk of compromise. Be judicious with these calls. And with what you say over the next couple of days."

"I will. Can you do me a favor and send someone to check on my mom and brother? Make sure they're all right?"

"I'll see to it. Remember what I said about talking to anyone."

"I will. Thank you." She wasn't supposed to contact her family directly. Or leave any forwarding addresses. And she was supposed to tell as few people as possible that she was moving. But she had to tell Larry and Penny as well as her clients that she wouldn't be sticking around. But beyond that she wouldn't tell a soul. Not even Mike.

She was leaving.

Word traveled fast in a small town.

Mike hadn't heard from Trisha in the last two days. He'd been trying to give her some space after opening up to her about Marcy's death. He'd hoped she might tell him a little about herself as well. She hadn't. He thought if he waited for a week, maybe two, she'd start to trust him. That he'd gently press her again for information. If she was a battered wife, maybe she was afraid the bastard would find her.

He'd decided to give her time. They had plenty of it.

He certainly hadn't expected to hear she was pulling up stakes and moving on. He'd gotten four phone calls this morning. The first one had been from Clara's mother, frantic that her daughter would no longer have access to an equine therapist, and could he see if there was another one within a hundred miles? As soon as his mind had stopped reeling, he'd promised to look into it. The next three calls had been from colleagues, who'd also heard the news, wondering if Trisha could send them those reports they'd asked for before she left.

His hands drew into tight fists on his desk. She hadn't bothered to call him and let him know she was going. Had she already been thinking about it when they'd spent the night together?

His head thumped out an angry rhythm and his stomach burned from the acid pouring into it. She didn't owe him an explanation.

But he sure wanted one.

Ignoring the warning signals that urged him to calm down and think this through before doing something rash, he grabbed up the phone and dialed her number.

"Hello?" Larry's voice came over the phone, his harried tone obvious. This was one unhappy man.

"This is Dr. Dunning. Is Trisha there?"

"She's here. Wait." Curt and to the point. He'd bet Trisha had gotten an earful about something. Good. At least he wasn't the only one taken by surprise. It was pretty obvious that Larry must know, especially if Trisha was telling her clients.

A few seconds later she was there, her greeting sounding wary and tired.

"What the hell's going on, Trisha?"

"I'm going away for a while."

"A while." The thumping in his head grew stronger. "Don't you mean you're moving? For good? That's what you told Clara's mother."

"Okay. I'm moving."

No other explanation was offered. That was okay,

because he wasn't afraid to ask. "Why? Is this because of me?"

Silence met his question for several long seconds. Then her voice came back. "Yes."

Yes. He'd expected her to give him some song and dance about how it wasn't anything personal, that she'd been called away on an emergency, or that she had a sick mother to take care of. A lie. And as stupid as it was, he was mad that he hadn't gotten one—that she'd given him a brutal dose of the truth instead.

"I see. When will you leave?"

Another pause. "As soon as all the arrangements are made."

That made him sit up. It was a strange way to word things. Not "in a week." Not "tomorrow morning". But "as soon as all the arrangements are made", as if someone else was pulling all the strings. Were they? Had something happened?

"Are you in some kind of trouble, Trisha?" He went back to what the sheriff had said about her background. Maybe she really was running from something. Or someone. "Is this about your husband?"

"Please, don't, Mike. I'm leaving. That's the end of it."

Tell her you love her and see if it changes things.

Where the hell had that come from?

He wasn't sure, but it was the truth. He'd known it for the last week, maybe longer. He'd just been in denial. Until now. When it was too late.

If this was about him—about what they'd done together—wouldn't it be easier just to say, "Hey, sorry, but I really don't want to get involved. Let's be friends"? Why go to all the expense of moving? It just didn't add up. And yet she'd said it was because of him.

She was moving. Because of him.

It was the craziest thing he'd ever heard. "What about your horses? Laredo?"

Sarah was still recovering from the accident and wouldn't be able to ride for a while. But he couldn't see Trisha leaving them all behind.

"Laredo's being moved to another boarding facility." Her voice cooled. "As for my horses, what I do with them is my business."

She wouldn't sell them. Especially not Brutus. She and that grouchy horse seemed joined at the hip. But whatever her plans were, she wasn't going to share them with him. He could take a hint—especially when it came in the form of a two-by-four upside the head.

"Are you coming by the hospital before you go?"

"I—I don't think that would be wise."

So he didn't even merit a formal goodbye. So be it. Mike had never believed in chasing after someone who didn't want to be caught. So he wasn't even going to try.

"Okay. Well, have a good trip."

"Thanks. Goodbye."

Mike had to force the words past the sudden knot in his throat. "Goodbye, Trisha."

With that, he hung up the phone and dragged various file folders in front of him. It was time to put this chapter in his life firmly behind him. What better way to do that than to fill it with work. Lots and lots of work.

Two days later he was still going strong. Just coming out of surgery, he popped his phone off his belt and checked for messages.

Ray Chapman had texted him. Twice. Since when did

the sheriff text rather than leave a voice mail? Pressing a button, he retrieved the messages. They were identical.

Inf on hippo.Call. Imprtnt.

Inf on hippo?

What on earth…? Maybe the man should step away from the keypad. Or get a better set of glasses.

The air caught in his chest as he reread the message. Hippo. Hippotherapist.

He checked the time. The sheriff had left the second text almost forty-five minutes ago.

He hit the dial button on his phone and headed for his office. Maybe the sheriff had discovered whatever Trisha was hiding. It was a little too late, though, since she was leaving. Whatever it was, it no longer mattered. He'd wanted the information to safeguard his patients. That was no longer a concern as far as the hippotherapist went, since she wouldn't be working with them any more. Still, he needed to call his friend and tell him to forget about it.

"I was wondering when you were going to get back to me." His friend's gruff voice came through, not wasting time on niceties. Kind of par for the course where Ray was concerned.

"I was in surgery. About Trisha. Don't bother doing any more research because—"

"She's leaving. Yeah, yeah, yeah. I kind of gathered that from the number of cars out at her place."

"Cars?" What was he talking about?

"You remember those vehicles I told you about?"

Mike searched his memory banks. "I'm drawing a blank here."

"There were a couple of dark cars that rolled into town

with her. I didn't think anything of it until you asked me to check for warrants. Well, those same cars are back."

"What do you mean, back?"

The sheriff gave an irritated snort. "Just what I said. I was parked on Miller Road at the entrance to town when these two sedans drove past me, keeping a careful eye on their speed. Government issue, if you ask me. I followed 'em, and they led me straight to the hippotherapist's place. I didn't take down license plates last time, but I'm pretty sure they're the same two men, down to the government-issue haircuts." He paused. "I'm guessing they're here to take her in. She had to have been involved in something pretty big to warrant the big dogs."

Mike's heart seized. Take her in? She was either being arrested or...

I can't tell you. Her words from a week ago rang in his ears, and the significance finally struck him.

She hadn't said "I don't want to tell you" or "I won't" but "I *can't.*"

She'd also said she wasn't running from the law. So if she wasn't being arrested...why were there strange vehicles at her place?

As soon as the arrangements are made.

She wasn't being arrested. She was being moved.

"Thanks, Ray. Keep an eye on her place for me. I'm on my way."

He hit the parking lot at a sprint and climbed into his car, flooring the gas pedal as soon as he found an open stretch of road. For the first time he cursed the hospital's location and the time it took to travel back and forth. Fifteen minutes later he passed Sheriff Chapman's car and sped on by, taking the first right. A cloud of dust spewed from beneath his vehicle as he skidded onto the dirt road. He saw the sheriff pull in behind him then switch on his lights and siren and swerve into the next lane before moving past him. Instead of busting him for speeding, Ray appeared to be leading the way.

Three minutes later he'd spun into Trisha's driveway. Mike pulled in beside his friend and braked in a hurry. There were indeed two sleek black SUVs parked in the gravel lot beside the barn, as well as a horse trailer hooked up to Trisha's big truck. That's not what captured his attention, however. It was the two men in dark suits…guns drawn.

Pointed straight at his windshield.

The sheriff was already out of the car, holding up his badge and demanding to see some ID.

The men ignored him, although they put their guns back into the holsters strapped across their chests. One of them, a big guy with close-cut gray hair, moved over to talk to his friend. Mike stepped out of the car, keeping his eyes trained on the second man, who looked a little trigger happy to him.

Trisha came bursting from the house at a run, feet bare, a long white skirt flowing out behind her. "It's okay. I know them."

Mike wasn't sure if she was talking to the men or to him and the sheriff. It didn't matter. Seeing her again crushed the air from his lungs and set his heart racing.

It seemed all that work he'd been doing hadn't helped after all.

She hurried over to him. "Mike, what's going on?"

"I could ask you the same thing."

She gave a visible swallow, then her chin lifted, and she crossed her arms over her chest. "I already told you. I'm leaving."

"Are you in trouble with the authorities?"

Her head swung in a slow arc to the left and to the right.

Her eyes—puffy and red—held his. Despite her defiant posture, she didn't seem angry. She seemed composed. Resigned, even.

"You're not being arrested?"

She shook her head again. And he knew. Knew why she couldn't tell him. Knew why the men had drawn their guns the second they'd seen the sheriff and him barreling toward them. They expected someone to come for Trisha. To try to hurt her. Maybe even kill her.

Damn. He should have known. Should have figured it out.

He moved toward her, only to have her hold out her hand when he was about five feet away. "Mike, please, don't. It's better for everyone this way. I—I don't want anyone to get hurt because of who I am."

The burly guy with the crew cut swung round and strode toward Trisha, pointing a finger right at her chest. "Hey. Not another word. We talked about this."

Mike saw red. He grabbed the guy's arm, only to find himself flat on his back, his jaw feeling like it had been hit by a fifty-pound bag of cement.

Trisha was on her knees beside him in a second, cradling his head and waving off the man who stood over him with clenched fists. Her eyes filled with tears, spilling over and running down her cheeks. "I'm so sorry. I never meant for any of this to happen. You're right. My name isn't Trisha Bolton. It's—"

"No." He stopped her. "He's right. You shouldn't say anything else."

A flash of hurt went through her eyes, but she reached up and dashed the tears from her cheeks.

He took a deep breath. "I don't care who you are. All I know is that if you're leaving, I'm going with you."

Silence met his declaration. Even the oaf who'd just sucker-punched him seemed dumbfounded.

Mike wasn't sure where the words had come from, but he knew he meant them.

"You can't," Trisha whispered. "You'd have to give up everything you love—your career, your home, your life."

She hadn't said she didn't want him to go with her. She'd said he'd have to give up everything he loved.

"No, Trisha, I wouldn't." He lifted a hand to her face, ignoring the tightening of the guy's hands in front of him.

"Yes, you would." She seemed steadier now. Trying to firm up her resolve maybe. "And I can't allow that."

He smiled and slid his fingers down her throat. "You're operating under the false assumption that I love any of those things. I don't. The only thing I love is…you."

Her eyes widened. "What?"

The sheriff, who had been hanging back, now moved toward them, his hand on his own gun. "You want to press charges, Mike?"

The burly guy gave a harsh laugh. "You've got to be kidding me."

"I never kid about assault, son." Ray's eyes were cool, his mouth tight.

Crap, he wasn't joking. Mike got to his feet, even though he wanted nothing better than to stay in Trisha's lap and have her stare into his eyes. But he really wanted to do this out of the public spotlight. He reached down and helped her up as well. Turning to his friend, he placed a hand on his shoulder. "No harm done. I think we both want the same thing: to make sure Trisha's safe." He glanced at the man he guessed was a federal agent. "Is that right?"

The guy's jaw shifted from one side to the other before he answered. "That's right."

Mike kept hold of Trisha's hand. "I'm going to take her over to the barn for a few minutes so we can talk in private. If you all don't mind waiting here. I'd appreciate it."

The agent stepped in front of them. "Ms. Bolton?"

"It's okay. I'll go."

She allowed him to haul her to the barn, but once they ducked through the door she tugged her hand free. "You love me?"

"I was hoping to take things slow the other day, hoped that by telling you about Marcy you'd realize I wanted to deepen things between us. But then you panicked, and I realized I'd screwed things up. I didn't know how much until you said you were leaving."

"I was scared. Terrified. If I told you who I was I could put you—as well as my family—in danger. Roger could try to find me through you. Or he could hurt you just to get back at me." She must have seen his confusion, because she licked her lips. "You were right. I was married at one time. My ex-husband was with the Russian mob, although I didn't know that when I married him. Long story short, I testified against him, and they put me into witness protection. The only thing real about me are my horses. Everything else is made up."

"Not everything. I fell in love with you. Not your alias." He realized something. "You haven't said how you feel."

She reached up and looped her arms around his neck. "I was willing to give it all up. This town, my patients. For you. Does that give you some idea?"

It did. But he didn't want any misunderstandings. "It's not only women who need the words, Trisha."

She laughed and kissed his jaw. "Okay, then. I love you. Better?"

"Better." His heart swelled, telling moisture gathering behind his eyes. He clenched his jaw, forcing the tide back. "So where are we off to? Mexico? The Dominican Republic? I kind of like the idea of you sprawled on a beach in a tiny bikini."

"How about staying right here?"

"Won't you be safer elsewhere?"

She shook her head. "I wasn't worried about me in the first place. I was worried about you. About my family."

"You have parents? Do you talk with them?"

"My father's dead, but I have a mother and a brother. No, I don't talk to them. They know I'm safe, but they don't know where I am or my new name. Someday maybe that will change, but for now I'm okay with it as long as they're not in any danger."

A horse neighed in the distance. Trisha's head turned in that direction. "I need to know something. Are you going to be okay with my profession, and about keeping secrets from people? I know with your wife…is it going to bother you?"

Mike thought through that for a second. Tried to piece together his jumbled emotions about Marcy and their last few months together. "I think I still need to work though some things. When what I felt for you became greater than my fears about the past, I knew I was in trouble."

"Maybe we should talk to someone about it. Because I plan to stick around for a long time."

He gathered her hair into a ponytail and tipped her head back to look in her eyes. "That sounds like a plan, because I'm going to hold you to sticking around. I might even let you give me some more lessons."

"That sounds perfect."

"So we're all in this together? The Feds and the horses and the secret agent lifestyle?"

"Definitely together. That's the only way I want to do this."

One of the horses' noses appeared over the door of a stall and regarded them before he cocked his head and let out a long shrill whinny that echoed throughout the barn.

Trisha laughed. "I think Brutus might just agree."

EPILOGUE

"ARE YOU SURE?"

Mike, coffee cup halfway to his mouth, stopped to consider her question. She held up a finger to let him know she'd be with him in a minute.

Her contact at the FBI was on the phone, letting her know that Roger, aka Viktor Terenovsky, had attempted to escape while being transferred to another prison and had been killed by police officers at the scene. "We're sure. It's over, Trisha."

Over. She glanced at her husband and then at the new high chair that was parked beneath the kitchen table. Happy hands were busy smearing morning oatmeal over the white plastic tray and a dot of the stuff clung to long dark lashes that looked very much like her daddy's. The tiny blob bounced up and down with every blink of her eyes. Abigail Cardoso Dunning had been born in the middle of a snowstorm—a rarity in these parts. Luckily her dad was a brain surgeon and had been able to figure out how to deliver her at home, even if his hands shook as he held his baby girl for the first time. She motioned to Mike tapping her own finger to her eyelashes and then pointing at Abby.

Mike grinned and set down his coffee and grabbed a napkin, attempting to wipe off the offending spot. Only

Abby acted as if the square of paper were some terrible monster, twisting her head to and fro to avoid being touched by it.

No, sweetheart, it's not a monster. The real bad guy will never be able to knock on your door...or pose a threat to you.

"I hate to say I'm relieved he's dead," she told Clyde. "But I am."

That got Mike's attention. He stared at her with enough force that she covered the handset with her palm. "Roger was killed last night while trying to escape."

"Wow. After five years. I thought his ghost would always be hanging around our doorstep."

The Feds had been pretty unhappy about Trisha staying in Dusty Hills and spilling the details of the situation to Mike, but she'd refused to keep any more secrets from this man. Once it had been out, the two agents had had no choice but to accept her decision to stay. They'd even promised to check in on her mom and brother periodically. And Ray had assured them that the town was pretty protective of its residents. No one else needed to know but them, and he'd keep a personal watch over the place. If someone so much as cruised past Trisha's driveway, he'd make the call himself. No one ever had. The two of them—three now, with Abby—had stayed put, and Trisha finally felt like she could safely put down roots. Maybe now she'd even be able to call her mom and introduce her to her granddaughter.

Trisha thanked the agent, knowing this was probably the last time she'd ever hear from him. "I appreciate everything you've done for me."

"You know," Clyde said, "you can probably even go back to using your old name if you want."

Patty Ann Stoker. That name seemed to come from

another era, belonging to another woman. Her life was far removed from her upper-crust roots back in New York City.

She glanced at Mike, who'd finally succeeded in wiping the oatmeal from Abby's mouth and eyelashes. She smiled. "I happen to love the name I have." *And the man who had given it to her.* "I think I'm going to keep it."

* * * * *

Mills & Boon® Hardback
August 2014

ROMANCE

Zarif's Convenient Queen	Lynne Graham
Uncovering Her Nine Month Secret	Jennie Lucas
His Forbidden Diamond	Susan Stephens
Undone by the Sultan's Touch	Caitlin Crews
The Argentinian's Demand	Cathy Williams
Taming the Notorious Sicilian	Michelle Smart
The Ultimate Seduction	Dani Collins
Billionaire's Secret	Chantelle Shaw
The Heat of the Night	Amy Andrews
The Morning After the Night Before	Nikki Logan
Here Comes the Bridesmaid	Avril Tremayne
How to Bag a Billionaire	Nina Milne
The Rebel and the Heiress	Michelle Douglas
Not Just a Convenient Marriage	Lucy Gordon
A Groom Worth Waiting For	Sophie Pembroke
Crown Prince, Pregnant Bride	Kate Hardy
Daring to Date Her Boss	Joanna Neil
A Doctor to Heal Her Heart	Annie Claydon

MEDICAL

Tempted by Her Boss	Scarlet Wilson
His Girl From Nowhere	Tina Beckett
Falling For Dr Dimitriou	Anne Fraser
Return of Dr Irresistible	Amalie Berlin

4GEN STD HB

Mills & Boon® Large Print
August 2014

ROMANCE

A D'Angelo Like No Other	Carole Mortimer
Seduced by the Sultan	Sharon Kendrick
When Christakos Meets His Match	Abby Green
The Purest of Diamonds?	Susan Stephens
Secrets of a Bollywood Marriage	Susanna Carr
What the Greek's Money Can't Buy	Maya Blake
The Last Prince of Dahaar	Tara Pammi
The Secret Ingredient	Nina Harrington
Stolen Kiss From a Prince	Teresa Carpenter
Behind the Film Star's Smile	Kate Hardy
The Return of Mrs Jones	Jessica Gilmore

HISTORICAL

Unlacing Lady Thea	Louise Allen
The Wedding Ring Quest	Carla Kelly
London's Most Wanted Rake	Bronwyn Scott
Scandal at Greystone Manor	Mary Nichols
Rescued from Ruin	Georgie Lee

MEDICAL

Tempted by Dr Morales	Carol Marinelli
The Accidental Romeo	Carol Marinelli
The Honourable Army Doc	Emily Forbes
A Doctor to Remember	Joanna Neil
Melting the Ice Queen's Heart	Amy Ruttan
Resisting Her Ex's Touch	Amber McKenzie

0714 GEN STD LP

ROMANCE

The Housekeeper's Awakening	Sharon Kendrick
More Precious than a Crown	Carol Marinelli
Captured by the Sheikh	Kate Hewitt
A Night in the Prince's Bed	Chantelle Shaw
Damaso Claims His Heir	Annie West
Changing Constantinou's Game	Jennifer Hayward
The Ultimate Revenge	Victoria Parker
Tycoon's Temptation	Trish Morey
The Party Dare	Anne Oliver
Sleeping with the Soldier	Charlotte Phillips
All's Fair in Lust & War	Amber Page
Dressed to Thrill	Bella Frances
Interview with a Tycoon	Cara Colter
Her Boss by Arrangement	Teresa Carpenter
In Her Rival's Arms	Alison Roberts
Frozen Heart, Melting Kiss	Ellie Darkins
After One Forbidden Night...	Amber McKenzie
Dr Perfect on Her Doorstep	Lucy Clark

MEDICAL

A Secret Shared...	Marion Lennox
Flirting with the Doc of Her Dreams	Janice Lynn
The Doctor Who Made Her Love Again	Susan Carlisle
The Maverick Who Ruled Her Heart	Susan Carlisle

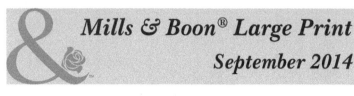
Mills & Boon® Large Print
September 2014

ROMANCE

The Only Woman to Defy Him	Carol Marinelli
Secrets of a Ruthless Tycoon	Cathy Williams
Gambling with the Crown	Lynn Raye Harris
The Forbidden Touch of Sanguardo	Julia James
One Night to Risk it All	Maisey Yates
A Clash with Cannavaro	Elizabeth Power
The Truth About De Campo	Jennifer Hayward
Expecting the Prince's Baby	Rebecca Winters
The Millionaire's Homecoming	Cara Colter
The Heir of the Castle	Scarlet Wilson
Twelve Hours of Temptation	Shoma Narayanan

HISTORICAL

Unwed and Unrepentant	Marguerite Kaye
Return of the Prodigal Gilvry	Ann Lethbridge
A Traitor's Touch	Helen Dickson
Yield to the Highlander	Terri Brisbin
Return of the Viking Warrior	Michelle Styles

MEDICAL

Waves of Temptation	Marion Lennox
Risk of a Lifetime	Caroline Anderson
To Play with Fire	Tina Beckett
The Dangers of Dating Dr Carvalho	Tina Beckett
Uncovering Her Secrets	Amalie Berlin
Unlocking the Doctor's Heart	Susanne Hampton

0814 GEN STD LP

MILLS & BOON®

Why shop at millsandboon.co.uk?

Each year, thousands of romance readers find their perfect read at millsandboon.co.uk. That's because we're passionate about bringing you the very best romantic fiction. Here are some of the advantages of shopping at www.millsandboon.co.uk:

* **Get new books first**—you'll be able to buy your favourite books one month before they hit the shops

* **Get exclusive discounts**—you'll also be able to buy our specially created monthly collections, with up to 50% off the RRP

* **Find your favourite authors**—latest news, interviews and new releases for all your favourite authors and series on our website, plus ideas for what to try next

* **Join in**—once you've bought your favourite books, don't forget to register with us to rate, review and join in the discussions

Visit **www.millsandboon.co.uk**
for all this and more today!